Samuel French Acting Edition

I0591761

Tin Cat Shoes

by Trish Harnetiaux

ISBN 978-0-573-70839-8

www.ConcordTheatricals.com
www.ConcordTheatricals.co.uk

FOR PRODUCTION ENQUIRIES

UNITED STATES AND CANADA
Info@ConcordTheatricals.com
1-866-979-0447

UNITED KINGDOM AND EUROPE
Licensing@ConcordTheatricals.co.uk
020-7054-7200

Each title is subject to availability from Concord Theatricals, depending
upon country of performance. Please be aware that *TIN CAT SHOES*
may not be licensed by Concord Theatricals in your territory.
Professional and amateur producers should contact the nearest
Concord Theatricals office or licensing partner to verify availability.

MUSIC USE NOTE

IMPORTANT BILLING AND CREDIT REQUIREMENTS

TIN CAT SHOES was first produced by Clubbed Thumb (Maria Striar, Producing Artistic Director; Michael Bulger, Associate Artistic Director) at The Wild Project in New York, New York on May 19, 2018. The performance was directed by Knud Adams, with sets by Kimie Nishikawa, costumes by Sydney Maresca, lights by Oona Curley, and sound by Peter Mills Weiss. The production stage manager was Corinn Moreno. The cast was as follows:

REX / THE BEAR / THE CROUPIER	David Greenspan
LUNCH / DANNY	Pete Simpson
GEMMA	Emily Cass McDonnell
PEPPER	Donetta Lavinia Grays
CHEDDAR	Kyle Beltran

CHARACTERS

Age, race, gender can be interchangeable
Pronouns should be changed according to casting

REX (and **THE BEAR** and **THE CROUPIER**) – owner of the shoe store, leader of the troops, worked for years as a customer service representative

LUNCH (and **DANNY**) – always giving the hint of a huge life lived, just beyond the surface of what we see

GEMMA – the new employee with a past full of holes

PEPPER – casually surprised not to be doing something else by now

CHEDDAR – magically content wherever he is

ROGER, THE UPS DELIVERY PERSON – voice-over

NARRATOR / 911 – voice-over

SETTING

Part One:
The Craigslist Hambone Story is in the shoe store.

Part Two:
The Bear is in the wilderness.

Part Three:
The Casino is in the casino.

TIME

Now.

AUTHOR'S NOTES

In **Part One**, everyone is completely genuine and happy. There is no judgment of one another – every sentence, every action, should be in the spirit of community. Even if the language appears to be judging or showing irritation – it's not. Everything should be in the spirit of extreme kindness. This conceit unravels after **Part One**.

In **Part Two**, time should feel a little like taffy in a taffy stretching machine.

Part Three is everything you want it to be, and more.

NOTE ON THE "TIN CAT FUGUE"

Cheddar's character has written this song. He is not a professional songwriter nor are they professional singers. If they happen to be good singers, wonderful. Though not necessary. It should have the sense of going on too long. It should be calibrated that certain lines and people are heard at different times so it's not complete chaos. But if it is complete chaos? As long as they are laser focused and into it and "acting" the role in a way that differs from their character, well, that's all we can hope for. There should be a real sad cheerfulness to it. Not sad to them, cheerful to them. You get it.

NOTE ON OPTIONAL MUSIC

An optional "Tin Cat Orchestral" audio track is available to licensees through Concord Theatricals. Please contact your licensing representative for rental information. "Tin Cat Orchestral" provides underscoring accompaniment for the **Prologue** (page 9).

THE TIN CAT SHOE(S) EMPLOYEE HANDBOOK

"The Tin Cat Shoe(s) Handbook, for Employee Eyes Only," is made available to all licensees upon receipt of payment for their performance license. Please contact your Concord Theatricals licensing representative for more information.

This play is partially based on a True Story and partially based on a Shoe Store. Basically, it's based on a Shoe Story.

"The beginning is always today."
– Mary Wollstonecraft

PROLOGUE

(The sound of birds on a lovely day.)

(Optional, "Tin Cat Orchestral"* to underscore the following.)

NARRATOR. THEY SAY IT WAS A GOOD YEAR TO WORK IN A SHOE STORE,

AND THE EMPLOYEES OF TIN CAT SHOES FELT IT UNDENIABLY.

THEY ANTICIPATED THE ARRIVAL OF THE AERO NORDIC BOOT WHICH WAS SUPPOSED TO,

IF EVERYTHING WENT RIGHT IN THE NORDIC COUNTRIES,

ARRIVE THIS VERY WEEK

(IF NOT THIS VERY DAY.)

BUT OUR STORY STARTS BEFORE THE SHOE ARRIVES,

BEFORE THE EXCURSION THAT LED TO THE MEETING WITH THE BEAR,

BEFORE THE DISAPPEARANCE OF REX,

AND WAY BEFORE THE WILD EVENTS THAT TOOK PLACE LATER THAT NIGHT AT THE CASINO...

WE FIRST MEET THEM EARLIER THAT MORNING,

WHEN THEY TOLD THE CRAIGSLIST HAMBONE STORY TO GEMMA,

ON HER FIRST DAY OF WORK...

---

* See page 6 for the Note on Optional Music.

PART ONE:
THE CRAIGSLIST HAMBONE STORY

(Shortly before Christmas, at Tin Cat Shoes.)

(Taking up a large portion of the stage is the Solo Shoe pile that **GEMMA** *and* **CHEDDAR** *are sorting through. Leisurely, they find matching pairs, wrap them in tissue paper, then place them in shoe boxes before stacking them neatly on a shelf.)*

(Perhaps soft shoe store music plays, Beach Boys instrumentals. **LUNCH**'s reading a magazine with some douche like Mark Zuckerberg on the cover.)*

CHEDDAR. *(To* **GEMMA.***)* Don't worry. I knew *nothing* about shoes when I started.

LUNCH. He didn't.

GEMMA. I respect their…importance. In protecting the feet.

CHEDDAR. You know what a shoehorn is yes?

GEMMA. Y –

CHEDDAR. When I started? I thought / a shoehorn –

LUNCH. *(Smiling.)* Don't say it.

CHEDDAR. Was a horn that sounded like a shoe.

> *(**LUNCH** lazily covers his ears.)*

> *(**CHEDDAR** opens his mouth and a huge sound like a ship's fog horn comes out.)*

> *(**GEMMA** covers her ears.)*

> *(**LUNCH** shakes his head.)*

LUNCH. *(Smiling and sincere.)* That was a fog horn.

---

* A license to produce *Tin Cat Shoes* does not include a performance license for any third-party or copyrighted recordings. Licensees should create their own.

(**CHEDDAR** *holds up a grumpy gold pump.*)

CHEDDAR. Who's got a grumpy gold pump?

(**GEMMA** *scans the pile and reaches for its match.*)

GEMMA. Gold pump!

CHEDDAR. Thanks.

LUNCH. We know this must feel –

CHEDDAR. And look.

LUNCH. – that this must feel and look *intimidating.*

(**LUNCH** *has said this with great compassion and caring.*)

CHEDDAR. New shipments <u>are</u> like this.

LUNCH. And, let's also face it.

This job, "*one*'s job," always has challenges.

GEMMA. I didn't realize... New inventory came this way.

LUNCH. It does, here.

Rex has his sources.

CHEDDAR. He's way more than,

you know,

just his fancy Leatherman.

GEMMA. What's a / Leather-man –

LUNCH. True, he talks about his Leatherman a lot,

we presented it to him after he won the Olympics last year –

GEMMA. He won the Olympics?

LUNCH. The *Tin Cat* Olympics.

It even has that cool engraving –

CHEDDAR. My cousin –

LUNCH. Cheddar's cousin is basically the *top* engraver.

But listen Gemma,

WE ALL HAVE DREAMS.

Cheddar even has a master's degree.

CHEDDAR. Feminist Literature.

LUNCH. Before this?

    Before her time at Whole Foods?

    Pepper wrote a *novel.*

CHEDDAR.	**LUNCH**.
Her novel was about her time at Whole Foods.	Everyone has a time.

CHEDDAR. Like, during a big storm.

LUNCH. Storm of the Century type of thing, you get it.

       (**GEMMA** *spots a solo green flat.*)

GEMMA. Green flat... Has anyone seen another green flat, left foot...women's size... eight?

CHEDDAR. No. Let's bet how long it takes to find / the other?

GEMMA. Oh no, no. I can't.

GEMMA. *(Quietly.)*	**LUNCH**.
I'm not supposed to bet anymore.	We don't really say "can't" around here.

GEMMA. What do we do with the solo ones?

LUNCH. Start a new pile.

GEMMA. Okay.

       (**GEMMA** *surveys the store and carefully selects the perfect place to start the new pile of Solo Shoes.*)

       (*She places the green flat on the floor delicately.*)

       (*She makes sure there's plenty of room around it for future shoes.*)

       (**CHEDDAR** *and* **LUNCH** *exchange a smile.*)

       (**LUNCH** *quickly identifies this as a compassionate teaching moment.*)

LUNCH. Not *there.*

GEMMA. Oh, okay.

LUNCH. Think about it.

GEMMA. Ohhhhh, okay. I will.

LUNCH. *The door.*

CHEDDAR. *La Puerta.*

LUNCH. That's directly in front of the door.

We can't just block it with the Solo Shoe Pile.

CHEDDAR. Because of *Access.*

LUNCH. Here, at Tin Cat Shoes,

we're constantly having to put ourselves in *situations*
Gemma.

Where we're thinking beyond the *Current Scenario.*

CHEDDAR. It's part of the *System.*

LUNCH. Say the Solo Shoe Pile grows out of control,

in the exact spot where you wanted to start it

with that green right flat of yours.

> (**LUNCH** *lovingly lets this sink in.*)

Cut to outside,

a family of four is walking down the street.

Laughing, holding hands, skipping, ice cream, no cares,
oh no,

it's snowing, oh no, FUCK.

CHEDDAR. *Boom.*

LUNCH. – they're in flip flops.

CHEDDAR. *Flip.*

Flop.

LUNCH. The mom – Carol –

> (*Pointing to* **CHEDDAR** *who is now* "Carol.")

– oh my god CAROL – *Carol* is so flustered.

> (*This is* **CHEDDAR**'s *goddamn dream to be
> playing* "Carol," *shit, he hasn't acted since he
> played Nicely-Nicely Johnson in* Guys *and*
> Dolls *his senior year of high school.*)

She hasn't anticipated this *Cold Turn.*

But, it's okay.

Little Carol Junior – the family scout – is by her side pointing,

pointing to a sign up ahead:

TIN CAT SHOES.

They're at the door, they're pulling –

CHEDDAR. Pushing.

LUNCH. – they're pushing –

> *(They push, really lean into it, in the way that the door won't open because something, something stupid, is certainly blocking it from the inside.)*

But oh no the door won't open, wait, is the store closed?

> *(**CHEDDAR** – as Carol – quietly echoes "Wait is the store closed?")*

Your shoe pile, Gemma, has blocked: An Access Point Called the Door.

Does it matter to them?

No, they leave.

Their feet are cold.

So, let's take that green flat to the other side of the store –

both for safety reasons and not to mention

the $172.80 Tin Cat did not make on the sale of four pairs of snow boots or,

translation, the $17.28 that's *not* in your paycheck.

LUNCH.	**CHEDDAR**.
For the commission.	For the commission.

GEMMA. Ohhhh, okay.

I wasn't sure how big the solo pile gets –

LUNCH.	**CHEDDAR**.
VERY big sometimes.	VERY big sometimes.

> *(Ha! They exchange dazzling looks!)*

Stop it ☺	Stop it ☺

(Eye-locked, they hesitate for only a moment, then:)

JINX!   JINX!

(Wouldn't it be awesome if they kept doing this all day?)

(They certainly think so.)

(Super-fast.) We've got to be top of our game when The Aero gets here.

(Super-fast.) One time the shipment was ALL Solo Shoes.

(LUNCH *claps* **CHEDDAR** *softly on the shoulder sensing that he's most disappointed they couldn't continue they're in-sync-speaking.)*

GEMMA. Sure.

CHEDDAR. Nice!

GEMMA. Does Rex own this place?

CHEDDAR. *Relevance.*

GEMMA. What?

LUNCH. Relevance *Theory 101.*

CHEDDAR. *Relevance.*

LUNCH. Cheddar sometimes speaks with one word. Don't take it personally. It's how he, how he conserves energy.

CHEDDAR. *Absolutely.*

LUNCH. Like he can be in the middle of a conversation or be describing something, anything, something simple even, and he knows when the tidal wave of exhaustion is coming, and he makes these adjustments in order, well, so that he doesn't...run out.

CHEDDAR. Yep.

LUNCH. It's genius. I help whenever I can, try to pick up where he is in a story. You get it. He appreciates it.

CHEDDAR. I do.

LUNCH. Even told me in a card one time, a card with my name on the front which –

LUNCH.   **CHEDDAR.**

  – was <u>underlined.</u>   – was <u>underlined.</u>

    (Beat.)

GEMMA. So no one knows who owns it?

CHEDDAR. We've never asked.

GEMMA. Really?

LUNCH. Boundaries I guess. We only ask Rex questions about things that directly affect us.

CHEDDAR. Are we open on Labor Day?

LUNCH. How do I lock the bathroom door?

CHEDDAR. Are we open on Presidents' Day?

  It's none of our business if Rex "owns the place or not" because we still only get paid every other Friday. We just have to find a way to work with him, and, together. It's a great System.

LUNCH. It's proven.

CHEDDAR. You'll get it. He's...a Systems Guy. And so's our team-family. It's important to have foundations, so, it's all about Systems. Shoe Systems.

GEMMA. Shoe Systems.

LUNCH. Gemma, we get a lot of applicants.

  And not just because of our location.

CHEDDAR. All the foot traffic.

  No pun / intended.

LUNCH. Gemma...yours really stood out.

GEMMA. It did?

CHEDDAR. Rex reads applications very closely and he has a System as we mentioned,

  even when it comes to New Hires.

LUNCH. Uh, I'd say *especially* when it comes to New Hires.

CHEDDAR. *Especially.*

  We're not consulted until the final stage.

  He...and well, *we*, noticed...

    (**CHEDDAR** *is excited...*)

(Looks at **LUNCH***...)*

*(***LUNCH*** smiles and nods.)*

There was a rather large gap in your Employment History.

*(***GEMMA*** freezes.)*

Rex is... Pro-gap.

GEMMA. Has anyone seen a dark brown men's loafer, right foot, size ten?

LUNCH. Pro-gap!

GEMMA. I'm fully prepared to commit to this job. To my co-workers. Actually, I'm hoping this isn't just a holiday employment opportunity.

LUNCH. Gemma, we're on your side!

GEMMA. Because I need the struc –

CHEDDAR. Lunch! It just hit me – I bet Gemma's never heard of a "floating crap game."

(Hums a few bars.)

Man, I had the *best* number.

(Twirls.)

Sometimes you don't have to be the star.

You just need to have *the stuff.*

LUNCH. The *number.*

CHEDDAR. I had the *number.* It's so funny what you remember right? Father Hamlen would say,

"Ched, you want people walking out the door humming *your song,*

not Richie from Algebra's song."

LUNCH. Ha.

GEMMA. I've spent, let's just say "a ton" of time, in casinos.

CHEDDAR. I'm talking about a song from a play about *the odds.*

LUNCH. Tell her about the talent show.

GEMMA. My brother –

– he held the dice once for *fifty-three minutes.*

CHEDDAR. I taught the troops, for the talent show.
We need Pepper to tell it.

LUNCH.   **GEMMA**.
    PEPPER!   Do you know what
                                       happens when you hold
                                       the dice that long?

CHEDDAR.
    Here's the deal,
    in a Floating Craps
    Game,
    I doubt that's
    encouraged.
    You gotta be real careful, **LUNCH**.
    cops / and stuff.   Law enforcement.

GEMMA. The crowds grew bigger and bigger
    and everyone kept laughing
    but nothing could touch that hot string of luck...
    You know?

LUNCH. Gemma, I'm talking about a *Floating Craps Game*,
    down on one knee –

CHEDDAR. – looking over your shoulder,
    pulling your hat down type stuff.
    You get it.

LUNCH. Frankly, it's easier to just show you.

CHEDDAR. PEPPER!

            (**PEPPER** *enters.*)

LUNCH. *Tin Cat Fugue.*

PEPPER. I'm a little rusty.

LUNCH. We really need to show Gems.

GEMMA. Gemma.

PEPPER. Did they tell you about first place? About the
    trophy?

GEMMA. No –

CHEDDAR. Let's show her!
    (*To* **GEMMA**.) I had to change the song.

PEPPER. Don't judge us –

CHEDDAR. Laws and such. Wrote us a new one.

PEPPER. – we haven't done this in ages.

CHEDDAR. To please the authorities.

LUNCH. Doesn't hurt to play by the rules!

CHEDDAR. *(Smiles.)* You can say that again.

PEPPER. Don't judge us, we haven't done this in *ages*.

> (**LUNCH** *rips some pages from the magazine he's been reading and hands them out as fake-racing-form-props.* **PEPPER**, **LUNCH**, *and* **CHEDDAR** *quickly do a whisper-regroup and get into position. The choreography of this section is very precise.* **CHEDDAR** *mimics the sound of a trumpet, the one it makes at the start of a horse race.)*

[MUSIC: "TIN CAT FUGUE"]

CHEDDAR.

PAUL REVERE IS
MY HORSE, HE'S
GRANDMASTER OF THE
COURSE.
ANY SUCKER WITH A
BUCK KNOWS HE IS PURE
EQUESTRIAN FORCE.

CHEDDAR.	PEPPER.
IT'S	**PEPPER.**
TRUE, IT'S TRUE.	MY FRONT RUNNER IS VALENTINE,
ALL THE PAPERS SAY HE'S A HULLABALOO.	SHE HAS GOT A GREAT BLOODLINE.
IT'S TRUE, IT'S TRUE.	YOU CAN SEE BY HER POSTURE
BET ON MY LIFE HE'LL NEVER BE GLUE.	SHE HAS GOT A PERFECT SPINE.

CHEDDAR.	PEPPER.	LUNCH.
MY BOOKIE GAVE ME AN INSIDE TIP:	SO SLICK, SO SLICK.	WHAT ABOUT DARLING EPITAPH?

CHEDDAR.	PEPPER.	LUNCH.
PAUL REVERE RAKES IN MORE LOOT THAN A PIRATE SHIP.	SHE'S HALF SAUDI – HALF BOLSHEVIK	SHE'S HALF MUSTANG – HALF GIRAFFE.
HE'S BEEN KNOWN TO SHRED THE MORNING LINE.	SO SLICK, SO SLICK.	IF YOU GOT A BIG OL' WAD O' CASH
AND DOES IT ALL WITH WORLDLY STATESMANSHIP	SHE LIKES A SLOPPY TRACK, SHE'S PERFECT A PICK.	YOU CAN GET HER AUTOGRAPH
HAS CLASS, HAS CLASS.	THE MICROSCOPIC JOCKEY ON VALENTINE,	SHE'S GOT GAME, GOT GAME.
MAKE SURE TO WATCH HIM WIN ON THE SIMULCAST.	ORIGINALLY FROM LIECHTENSTEIN	HER VICTORY IS SWEETER THAN ASPARTAME
HAS CLASS, HAS CLASS.	HAS A TEENY TINY MOUTH THAT NEVER SMILES.	SHE'S GOT GAME, GOT GAME.
SMOKES THE COMPETITION LIKE MUSTARD GAS.	KINDA LOOKS LIKE DOCTOR FRANKENSTEIN –	SHE PAYS OUT MORE THAN AN INSURANCE CLAIM.

LUNCH. *The race is about to start –*

PEPPER. Alright, alright. I think she gets it.

GEMMA. That was...great.

> (**CHEDDAR** *and* **LUNCH** *high five with some "whoop whoops!")*

PEPPER. First place.

GEMMA. That's so...cool.

PEPPER. We do a lot of fun things around here.

GEMMA. Yeah, seems like it.

PEPPER. Hey, has Cheddar told you The Craigslist Hambone Story yet?

LUNCH. Great idea! Actually, let me tell it.

PEPPER. Yeah?

LUNCH. Come on, I've *never* told it. I've *always* wanted to –

CHEDDAR. Let Lunch tell it.

LUNCH. Yesssss.

Okay, let's see.

Cheddar's sitting there,

after Easter Dinner last year.

CHEDDAR. Three years ago.

LUNCH. Woah –

(Huge genuine incredulous smile.)

Really?

CHEDDAR. Yeah.

LUNCH. Man, Okay.

Three years ago, there is Ched,

just sitting there at Easter Dinner.

Someone cooked or bought –

CHEDDAR. My cou / sin –

LUNCH. His cousin cooked this Big Ham and it was de-licious.

CHEDDAR. It was *delicious.*

LUNCH. They used honey *and* sage I believe?

(CHEDDAR's impressed with LUNCH's attention to detail in his retelling.)

CHEDDAR. Ha! Honey and sage.

LUNCH. Blah, blah, chomp, chomp, so now it's *after* dinner –

PEPPER. *(But, with love.)* Man, you are terrible / at this.

LUNCH. And Ched gets struck by...one of... Those Moments. You know.

GEMMA. He's tired?

PEPPER. He gets these other moments.

CHEDDAR. I do.

LUNCH. Usually, right after he's eaten a big meal.

CHEDDAR. I want to help the world.

LUNCH. He wants to help the world.

CHEDDAR.	**LUNCH.**
In these moments,	To help the entire world.
I have a strong desire...	

LUNCH. He wants to help humanity.
    Make the Earth a better place.
    See, Cheddar believes in Karma, always has.
    And, in composting.

CHEDDAR. Karma and composting.

GEMMA. What?

LUNCH. And usually, after a meal, is when he starts identifying – hard core – with the less fortunate.

CHEDDAR. Lessers.

PEPPER. But, meanwhile...

LUNCH. But, meanwhile... He's a shitty dinner guest –

CHEDDAR. I am.

LUNCH. Has done nothing to help whatsoever –

CHEDDAR. At all.

> (**PEPPER** *finds the other green flat in the Shoe Pile.*)

LUNCH. Is pretty drunk –

CHEDDAR. Kinda smashed.

LUNCH. And this is when, this cold Easter night three years ago, he focuses in on...The Hambone.

> (**GEMMA** *eyes the flat in* **PEPPER**'s *hand.*)

GEMMA. Is that a green flat size eight?

> (**PEPPER** *flips it to* **GEMMA**.)

PEPPER. Baby's first match!

*(**GEMMA** goes and removes the other green flat
from what would have been the beginning of
the Solo Shoe Pile.)*

*(She takes the pair, folding them carefully
and places them, tidily, in the shoe box.)*

LUNCH. The Hambone, the pearl of the plate.

PEPPER. Ched doesn't...

come across very, ah,

positive in this story.

CHEDDAR. Uh, *correct.*

*(**PEPPER** and **CHEDDAR** high five!)*

LUNCH. But you can't argue,

it's important she hear it.

Ched-dawg decides –

he's going *to give it away.*

GEMMA. The Hambone.

CHEDDAR. The Hambone.

LUNCH. Just, poof, / give it away.

PEPPER. *Poof.*

GEMMA. To save humanity?

LUNCH. Pork makes him very generous.

PEPPER. True, it makes him nicer.

GEMMA. Nicer because he wants to give / The Hambone –

LUNCH. Give The Hambone –

GEMMA & LUNCH. Away.

CHEDDAR. I was making a stand.

Against...waste.

LUNCH. Back to The Hambone.

Now here's the part where we highlight what may
actually be the *true origin* of his generosity.

All his friends were leaving on a trip the next day.

And there wasn't a big enough

I'M PRETTY SURE

a big enough FREEZER BAG for The Hambone.
Say, if they wanted to keep it to make soup later,
or when they got back from their trip even.

CHEDDAR. That wasn't it.

LUNCH. *(Kind and wondrous.)* Really??

CHEDDAR. They had HUGE freezer bags.

Biggest I'd ever seen.

I knew it would fit. The revelation came in realizing: hey, *I hope it doesn't fit.*

Fitting wasn't what I was interested in.

Or concerned about.

You guys remember *Schindler's List*?

That scene when Ralph Fiennes is on the balcony or whatever and has his gun and can just kill anyone he wants at any moment? But Liam Neeson, née *Schindler,* is like –

the power is in *knowing you can,*

and choosing not to, my friend.

Or, I don't think he said, "my friend"...

What I was concerned about was trying to do something different.

Bigger than us. Bigger than my cousin even.

I was trying to fill this giant hole in myself.

There I was, eating ham ALL night

and then it was just me and that Hambone.

PEPPER. Kinda breaks my heart.

CHEDDAR. It was... *Devastating* on some level.

LUNCH. Are you telling the story now?

CHEDDAR. Naw.

LUNCH. So, everyone's super full from dinner.

Everyone's going skiing the next day –

CHEDDAR. Burning Man. They were all going to Burning Man.

LUNCH. So, they're all going to Burning Man the next day.

Everyone's packing up booze and gathering socks and stuff

...and Cheddar is the last one at the table.

PEPPER. The Hambone.

LUNCH. Ched, and The Hambone.

And he's dead set

on finding a home

for the poor bone.

GEMMA. *(To PEPPER.)* I have no idea where this is going.

PEPPER. *(To GEMMA.)* Yeah, I can see that.

GEMMA. Does The Hambone like spring / to life or something?

PEPPER. So, he grabs his phone –

LUNCH. Cheddar grabs his phone!

He starts typing.

CHEDDAR. App.

LUNCH. Oh, he starts dictating into his little APP!

LUNCH.	**CHEDDAR.**
"I have a hambone I don't want, what do I do?"	"I have a hambone I don't want, what do I do?"

LUNCH. I won't bore you with the details on "how he came to write the ad,"

But, in the end, he went Craigslist –

GEMMA. Went Craigslist –

LUNCH. And within minutes

mere minutes

was doing Ye-Old-Back-and-Forth with an unknown who was,

apparently,

this is kismet,

searching the Free Section for...

A Hambone.

LUNCH, CHEDDAR & PEPPER. Jackpot.

LUNCH. It was this dude's day.

Hell, it was this *bone's day.*

(To **PEPPER**.*)* You be him.

PEPPER. Come on Lunch-bag.

     (Lunch-bag is **PEPPER***'s nickname for* **LUNCH**.*)*

LUNCH. "Do you want it?"

PEPPER. "Yes."

LUNCH. "Come get it."

PEPPER. "I can't come get it."

LUNCH. "Oh?"

PEPPER. "Something's happened. I can't leave the house."

LUNCH. "I understand."

PEPPER. "Can you bring it?"

LUNCH. Cheddar's like –

LUNCH.	**CHEDDAR**.
"Why not, right?"	"Why not, right?"

LUNCH. Hell,

Ched wasn't going to Burning Man the next day,

there wasn't enough room in the Smart Car!

This was a calling!

Why the heck not!

BUT...what's with this Plot Twist?

The Future Hambone Recipient was unable to travel to obtain The Hambone,

which is pretty customary in these sorts of interactions.

And now, The Future Hambone Recipient requests that The Hambone's Dad –

CHEDDAR. Which is me.

LUNCH. Which is Cheddar – that he drive it across town to drop it off.

CHEDDAR. Which, truthfully, was not part of the original scenario when I was visualizing.

LUNCH. ...Does he bring it?

GEMMA. He brings it?

LUNCH. He brings it.

(Romantic shift.)

PEPPER. "Thanks for bringing This Hambone."

LUNCH.	**CHEDDAR.**
"Not a problem."	"Not a problem."

PEPPER. "Didn't mean for it to be a hassle."

LUNCH. "Alright, well –"

("...What is this strange impulse... I don't want to go...")

"...Enjoy The Hambone sir."

PEPPER. *("Huh, unexpected emotion, I don't want this person to leave.")* "Wait!"

LUNCH. "Yes?"

PEPPER. "Do you like...

"Hambone soup?"

LUNCH. "I...with little potatoes? Peas?"

PEPPER. "Yes. Why don't you come back...for some?"

CHEDDAR. What actually happened was... *Extraordinary.*

(A loud Bird chirping alarm sounds.)

LUNCH. The birds!

CHEDDAR. He's doing this now?

GEMMA. What is that?

LUNCH. Group stuff.

Last week we watched *Casablanca.*

CHEDDAR. Sick movie.

PEPPER. Have you signed all the New Employee Forms?

GEMMA. Yes.

PEPPER. Welcome to your first expedition.

*(**LUNCH** and **CHEDDAR** exit to backroom.)*

PEPPER.	**GEMMA.**
Hope you have bear spray.	Did you like working at Whole Foods?

*(**PEPPER** loves talking about Whole Foods. She continues to sort shoes through the following.)*

PEPPER. Whole Foods?

Since you did ask,

I hope this doesn't sound like bragging

or trying to be different or shaming you guys,

because I'm not into shaming anymore,

but when I was working at Whole Foods,

way before Tin Cat,

I learned a lot.

And not only the normal stuff like facts

about Animal Welfare Quality Standards

or Anti-Pesticide Abortion Groups.

I mean more helpful statistics. Or, rather, *job* statistics

or *human resource types of operations* such as – ways

to demonstrate kindness to others

or – understanding our delivery circumference.

I'm also talking about lifestyle choices and understanding the instincts of *homo sapiens* because let's face it, we all face multiple realizations when confronting our mortality and this is most likely to occur at work since Americans spend roughly seventy-six percent of their lives there –

just ask my old boss.

If we don't look out for our colleagues?

If we wait to practice human decency until we're safely done with work?

Well, that's *animal.*

See? Cheddar doesn't have the market on social consciousness cornered.

There are a lot of things I could say right now about how to employ, or deploy, my knowledge received say in *one* work environment that I transferred into *another,*

perhaps different but equally treasured, work environment.

I could offer suggestions about rainy day apparel.

Review the benefits of eating enough protein.

Highlight my discoveries regarding nepotism.

But, back on track, that alarm you heard? Those birds? The reason I asked if you had bear spray with you? Is that, we're about to have a Tin Cat Troop Trip and we need be prepared.

See, I know about the diet of these Northern Bears which I'm happy to tell you about because,

at one point,

I worked the honey aisle for the weekend.

Just up and down that fucking honey aisle all day.

I wrote a killer short story about it.

But you know what I learned?

What I learned that bears like?

They like People.

> (**LUNCH** *and* **CHEDDAR** *return with shoe boxes in hand.*)

People taste really, really, really, good to them.

Honey and people.

Or people dipped in honey would probably be like their ideal.

You get it...

> (**REX** *enters.*)

> (*He holds a box.*)

REX. They're here.

LUNCH. The Aero?

REX. No word on The Aero yet.

PEPPER. All Systems ready sir!

REX. It's official. Troop-ware *has arrived.*

> (*No one besides* **REX** *even knew Troop-ware was coming.*)

> (**REX** *holds up a khaki button up shirt full of patches, it looks not unlike a Scout Troop Uniform.*)

LUNCH. Beautiful –

GEMMA. Uniform?

REX. I've been designing these for years.

I come from a long line of wartime fabric weavers.

This fabric? Each stitch along the seam, chosen for a reason, fulfilling a purpose.

> *(He pulls the shirts out one by one and tosses them to each.)*

Pepper. Lunch. Cheddar. Gemma. Try them on!

> *(Glancing around.)*

Where's the solo shoe pile?

LUNCH.	**GEMMA.**
You'll be happy to hear, initially, it was too near the door, but after an exercise in *Scenario Analysis* we moved the Solo Shoe Pile to the other side.	I made the initial pile. There was only the one green flat but we found the other and I wrapped them together in a box. So, now there is no pile.

REX. Excellent work Gemma, what would we do without you.

GEMMA. Pepper! Pepper found the match.

But still, so, now there's no Solo Shoe Pile at all. Sir.

REX. But now you know where it goes.

GEMMA. Correct.

REX. Pepper, is this true?

PEPPER. Yes.

The flat was merely hidden.

Not missing.

REX. *(Just beaming.)* Amazing work team.

You heard the birds, Pop-up outing.

It's practically spring out!

We're closing early.

Lock up your phones.

You won't need them.

Bring your eyes and ears and hearts.
Our last excursion of the year,
our first one with Gemma,
will be one for the books.
Can't think of a better way to welcome her to
The International Northern Cusp Alliance Troops.

GEMMA. *The International Northern Cusp Alliance Troops?*

REX. T.I.N. C.A.T.

GEMMA. Clever, not sure how I missed that, sir.

PEPPER. *(To* **GEMMA**.*)* You know the song?

GEMMA. I think so...

[MUSIC: "TIN CAT TROOP SONG"]

ALL.

WE ARE THE TIN CAT TROOPS
PACK 3-4-2-7-1
WE'RE LOYAL TO OUR FRIENDS AND DEN
UP TO THE VERY, VERY END! END! END!

PART TWO: THE BEAR

(An urgent phone call.)

911. 9-1-1, how can I help you?

GEMMA. We're out near the Yakima River Basin,
by the rocks that are probably,
we bet,
only *one* million years old.
Our Store Manager and Troop Marshall – Rex –

> *(Some muffled conferring "what was it again?" with the others.)*

His *formal name* is Rex Jeremy Johnson the Third?
Has been pulled into an old cave by a huge bear.
Before you ask,
none of us actually saw this bear,
but we are almost certain that he, that Rex,
must be curled up?
Underneath his The Ritz Carlton sweatshirt probably
in the fetal position.
Near the back of the cave.
Or where we think the back of the cave is...
totally possible it continues further.

911. Has there been a scuffle?

GEMMA. We have heard what sounds like –

> *(Some muffled conferring with the others.)*

– sounds like "large paws" "batting" around and
"occasionally" making contact with something "soft" or
"swollen"?

911. Flesh?

GEMMA. Possibly flesh?
We have to admit something now?
At this point, we're not sure...
See Rex was, is, a Systems Guy?

There's certain suspicion, *per my co-workers,*
that this could be a Systems Exercise?
It's totally possible this is an elaborate test of some sort,
perhaps of Cave Systems or –

    (Muffled conferring with the others.)

There could be testing of Bear Systems happening?

    (Beat.)

Basically, we know there's a charge for false calls and
for ambulance rides and none of us are prepared to
absorb the cost of those fees if this is all, say, not even
a real thing.

    (Beat.)

We're shoe store employees.

911. How long has he been missing?

GEMMA. An hour...

    Ten minutes...

    It's unclear, time has, has...

    (Makes a sucking noise.)

    Since he was...yanked in?

    It's been difficult for us to determine...

    You might not understand this analogy,

    but we feel like astronauts?

    Circumstances and time and next steps...

    The previous systems in place have been failing...

    It's been a disaster. We're falling apart?

    Between you and me, I think one of my co-workers is
living IN the shoe store and –

    *(Some louder muffled conferring with the
others, the phrase "no one lives in the shoe
store" amidst a scuffle for the phone, which*
PEPPER *wins.)*

PEPPER. Hey, hey, hey, hey, hey, hey, hi –
No one lives in the shoe store.

Rex always said one of the reasons he started his own Troop Faction in the first place

was his high level of suspicion when it comes to Authority so if you repeat that I'm pretty sure no one will believe you *especially not Rex.*

911. Rex from the cave.

PEPPER. Yes. Exactly.

911. Do you have a *location*?

PEPPER. This is one of the real shit parts of this whole situation.

We are CRAP at locations.

We know we're by the River Basin, but that's about it.

Hell, the only phone we have is this *burner* phone I'm on.

Couldn't even tell you the number.

911. What do you see?

PEPPER. Some fields.

Rock formations.

Mountain in the distance.

The goddamn sun's going down.

911. Could you make a Signal Fire?

PEPPER. Hold –

(Muffled conferring with others.)

We could try to make a Signal Fire...ish.

911. Make a signal fire.

PEPPER. Listen, I have some – albeit limited – experience with tranquilizer guns and I'm happy to step up if the situation needs it. If, for whatever reason, you're not able to reach us, by say Traditional Roads, one option might be to send in a chopper and *Air Drop* some *Tranq Guns.*

(Beat.)

There's no need to like call in a bunch of people if they're – off shift – is all I'm saying.

(Beat.)

I'm seriously happy to help.

(Beat.)

Hello?

(Beat.)

911?

(Beat.)

Shit, the phone's dead.

***

(In the wilderness.)

(Before.)

REX. It's wonderful, actually. Each winter,
the Northwest Mountain Bear sleeps for five months.

CHEDDAR. Lucky bear.

REX. *Hibernation* – it's a beautiful word.
Maternal.
Hi-ber-na-tion.
It rhymes with –
"This Great Nation"
Hibernation... This Great Nation.

> (**REX** *waits for a laugh, but no one even knew*
> *he was trying to make a rhyming joke.)*

If ONE were,
was,
writing,
a poem for instance,
they might choose to end the stanza with...
a rhyming word.
Or words.
As in...poetry.
Hibernation... "This Great Nation."
Does anyone know what the –

(All four of The International Northern Cusp Alliance Troops raise their hands immediately and eagerly.)

PEPPER. I know it Rex.

Just let me answer.

REX. PEPPER!

PEPPER. They eat people.

REX. Black Bears and Grizzly Bears and Northern Bears, yes, *have* been known to eat people.

PEPPER. They love eating people.

GEMMA. And Honey, remember?

I wonder if it's that combination of both savory and sweet.

Assuming, sir, that we...are the savory.

REX. Gemma, great critical thinking.

But, it's perfectly safe here.

They're sleeping.

GEMMA. But sir –

REX. Rex.

GEMMA. Rex, are you worried about global warming and the effects on rising temper –

REX. Okay everyone. What you see behind me, right here, this structure, this rock formation, it's been here for millions and millions of years. At least one million or perhaps three million – depending on who you ask.

(No one knows what to do with this.)

If you ask *me* – I see a lot of correlation, or, rather, evidence that somewhere around the fifty-million-year mark a great catastrophe hit our world causing chaos and plate tectonical upheavals all the way from Cleveland to Auckland, giving this structure its shape. From chaos comes opportunity. It's taken generations for us to band together, learn how to live, learn how to cooperate and grow as a team, and looking at rock structures such as these allow us that quiet moment we

unknowingly crave to really contemplate who we are
and what came before us.

CHEDDAR. Uh –

REX. It's moments like these where you can taste the history
of the world –

> (**REX** *casually pushes some sort of little button
> inside the pocket of his sweatshirt, playing
> his own underscoring music*.)*

– that you remember your entire life,

or my name isn't Rex Jeremy Johnson, the Third.

For over a thousand years I've been bringing Troops
like yourselves here –

Smart hot shots with futures brimming with potential,
with success.

> (*Motioning to the rocks and cave next to
> him.)*

See how the two rocks split to create a cavernous cave?

See the beauty of the mountains in the distance?

You might think,

since I'm a non-conformist Systems Guy

running a highly successful shoe store,

that I would be a neigh-slayer of tradition.

That it's only because I've created Applied Systems

from information culled from my numerous,

numerous years in Customer Service that I "know more."

That I'm "quicker" to identify a "Sweet Spot."

The reality? To keep humble and in touch,

I return to this cave every year.

And, this year, with <u>you</u> – Tin Cat Troops.

You guys feel it right?

It's in *recognizing* the hidden places that speak to us,

this cave,

---

* A license to produce *Tin Cat Shoes* does not include a performance
license for any third-party or copyrighted recordings. Licensees should
create their own.

our earth,

that we become closer to it.

GEMMA. To what?

REX. To greatness and purpose.

We only know who we truly are when tested.

The very foundation of which The International Northern Cusp Alliance Troops has been built, grew from this land.

GEMMA. Flowers growing from rocks, sir!

CHEDDAR. I think she's referencing an old feminist continuum theory that –

> (**REX** *slight panic-gasps like he's forgotten something.*)

REX. Where's my Leatherman?

> (*Finds it safely on his belt.*)

Here it is.

Okay.

I'll go in first,

reacquaint myself with the place.

Then each,

in your own time,

follow me.

Stand tall troops.

Breathe it in.

Circle up!

> (*They circle up, but hesitantly.*)

> (**REX** *breathes in the beauty that surrounds him.*)

This sun. That view. This cave.

> (**REX** *confidently sticks his arm into the crevice of the cave, pointing.*)

I've been coming here since I was small.

This cave my playground.

I was just a boy with a piece of chalk and a pair of
shoes.

I've never told anyone this,

but somewhere deep inside

there's an old chalk drawing:

the first business plan for Tin Cat.

See Troops, nothing can be accomplished without a
well thought through business plan,

and I knew tha –

> (**REX***'s body jerks suddenly, he disappears
> inside the cave.*)

> (*Gone.*)

> (*As if he was never there.*)

***

> (*Panicked silence.*)

PEPPER. Oh, no, no, no.

LUNCH. He's playing.

PEPPER. I don't...

GEMMA.	**CHEDDAR.**
Oh my god, I'm sorry?	Paw. Paw.
	Paw.
	Paw.
	Paw.
	Paw.
	Paw.
	Paw.
	Paw.

LUNCH. I didn't see a paw.

CHEDDAR. I saw a huge claw, furry-like paw, grab his arm.

GEMMA. I saw something.

LUNCH. How did I miss it?

GEMMA. Fast, it happened really fast.

PEPPER.	CHEDDAR.
He's not dead.	I bet he's already dead.
He's not dead?	

> (**GEMMA** *slaps her own face.*)

GEMMA. Is this real?

> (**GEMMA** *smacks herself across her face again.*)

CHEDDAR. Yes.

GEMMA. Is this...part of the outing?

LUNCH. Are you hitting yourself in the face?

PEPPER. Is that an existential question?

GEMMA. I'm sure you won't understand this, but sometimes I wake up *punching myself in the face.* I have a mark here, right here under my eye, it's little. I was asleep, or half asleep, and I was in this store, and this man, attacking me and, and, I went to punch him but hit my face since I was actually just...in bed.

CHEDDAR. If you're suggesting some hyper-psychological-theory like we're-not-even-here, please, spare us.

> (**PEPPER** *moves a little closer to the cave entrance and whisper yells:*)

PEPPER. Rex!

> (*Thump-thump-thump.*)

> (*They scatter.*)

> (*A strangled cry is heard, immediately silenced and followed by a thud.*)

LUNCH. Who secretly brought their phone?

> (*No one did.*)

> (**REX***'s military style knapsack is nearby.*)

GEMMA. Check Rex's bag?

> (**PEPPER** *grabs it and starts riffling, one hand inside, like a Christmas stocking.*)

> (*She pulls out a shoehorn.*)

PEPPER. A shoehorn.

>   *(Pulling out three Kind Bars.)*

   Three Kind Bars.

CHEDDAR. Peanut butter and Chocolate!

GEMMA. I'm an almond girl.

>   (**PEPPER** *pulls out what looks like ticker tape.)*

GEMMA. Is that Ticker Tape?

PEPPER. *(Reading.)* 0, 2, 14, 35, 23, 4, 16?

>   *(Beat.)*

   33, 21, 6, 18, 31, 19, 8?

CHEDDAR. Coordinates?

LUNCH. System Study?

PEPPER. 12, 29, 25, 10, 27, 00 –

CHEDDAR.	**PEPPER**.
Double zero??	Shoe Sizes? Systems?

PEPPER. 1, 13, 36, 24, 3, 15, 34, 22.

>   *(Nothing. No one knows.)*

GEMMA. Where's the handbook?

LUNCH. What handbook?

GEMMA. Who saw the paw?

CHEDDAR. Moi.

   Paw.

LUNCH. Have you guys ever seen those bear paws on a stick?

CHEDDAR. That's not a thing.

LUNCH. It's a thing that they have in like New Orleans / I believe.

CHEDDAR. Bear paws on sticks are not a thing.

LUNCH. They are actually *really popular* and men and women sell them at *parades* I believe.

CHEDDAR. Down in New Orleans?

>   *(Geographically that's not correct.)*

LUNCH. Actually, over, then down. In New Orleans.

CHEDDAR. Hey can you do yourself a favor and stop saying "actually" actually?

LUNCH. You have a lot of rules today –

> (**PEPPER** *feels a little light headed.*)

PEPPER. Team-troops: this is what I believe they'd call a *fucking nightmare*. It's exactly this sort of frontal lobe stress that leads to blood clots, aneurysms, and death.

GEMMA. Jesus, Pepper.

PEPPER. What? I'm experiencing a light, light headedness.

It's either that or we're all astronauts…

which I could make an argument for based on the landscape.

Ugh –

(To self.) – quiet imagination!

CHEDDAR. Gemma, we need to keep it together.

GEMMA. I didn't say anything!

> (**PEPPER**'s *still searching in the bag with her hand.*)

Where are we even?

Who's good with directions?

> *(No one is.)*

PEPPER. I think I found something –

> (**PEPPER** *pulls out a rhyming dictionary.*)

A rhyming dictionary!

> *(Flipping through.)*

Wait – how do you spell mustache?

LUNCH. It's like "stomach," but with an "M."

PEPPER. No, it's not.

LUNCH. I think I won a spelling bee before, it is.

PEPPER. *Lunch-bag.*

GEMMA. That's not right.

LUNCH. Uh, I think it *is* right.

> (**PEPPER** *pulls out a burner phone.*)

PEPPER. A phone!

LUNCH. Is that a burner phone?

PEPPER. It totally looks like a burner phone.

> (**LUNCH** *unwraps a Kind Bar and tosses it towards the cave.*)

CHEDDAR. We only have *three* Kind Bars.

LUNCH. Don't be *abstemious*.

> (**CHEDDAR** *looks at* **LUNCH** *in that way that says: "Friend you don't even know what abstemious means.")*

I'm going to lure it.

CHEDDAR. Lure it?

GEMMA. With a Peanut butter Kind Bar?

What sort of Shoe Store is this?

PEPPER. Calm down –

GEMMA. I won't calm down. *Abstemious.*

Give me that burner phone.

Why haven't we called 911?

CHEDDAR. We're a generation without urgency?

LUNCH. Make sure to use his full name.

CHEDDAR. Formally, he goes by Rex Jeremy Johnson the Third. R.J.J.

PEPPER. *(Meaning it.)* Oh, he'd love that.

LUNCH. He's very specific about *records*.

If there's a recording of the call, like there always is, and he happens to be very much alive later?

He'll be thrilled we remembered this detail about him.

PEPPER. Thrilled.

Big on details.

You guys, I need to propose a theory.

LUNCH. What?

PEPPER. It's not *implausible* that this, that the whole "my cave drawings that were the earliest version of what was to become the dynasty of Tin Cat Shoes" thing was part of some... System.

LUNCH. Like a plan?

PEPPER. 'Zactly. Like you can see it right?

GEMMA. What do you mean?

CHEDDAR. Gemma, it would be hardest for you to see it. Being as you're new.

GEMMA. Um, I'm pretty sure the reverse is true.

CHEDDAR.	**LUNCH.**
Pretty sure no.	Pretty sure no.

GEMMA. I'm the *one* that can actually SEE things. You are inside it, so that makes it harder to see it.

LUNCH. Is that a fact?

GEMMA. I'd consider that a pretty well known fact.

PEPPER. Say you're right.

GEMMA. One of those *Laws of Nature* type things.

PEPPER. Say we have no idea what's happening. Don't you think that Rex would already know that? That he would have *thought of that* as he was devising the system we're in?

GEMMA. This isn't the Milky Way! We're not in a system.

PEPPER. Uh, your analogies are shit.

LUNCH.	**CHEDDAR.**
That's a candy bar.	That's a galaxy.

LUNCH. Pep is right here. Rex knows us – a little too well. Full disclosure, his skills of anticipation are so heightened he usually knows what I say even before I say it.

GEMMA. So, you don't think there's a bear.

PEPPER. Not really.

CHEDDAR. Maybe.

LUNCH. Could go either way.

GEMMA. But you saw that, that large paw grab him?

LUNCH. New Orleans.

PEPPER. Rex has a lot of friends.

CHEDDAR. True.

GEMMA. You think that was a friend / of his??

PEPPER. Seriously Gemma –

GEMMA. Not a bear?

PEPPER. We're exploring the *options* right now. I think it's okay to do a little <u>Think Tanking</u>.

GEMMA. I'm not against it, but what are we think tanking?

PEPPER. Also, Lunch probably knows why I'm hesitating to call an ambulance...

(**LUNCH** *gasps.*)

LUNCH. Totalllllllly forgot about that.

PEPPER. *Yeah.*

LUNCH. Oh, wow.

(**CHEDDAR** *gasps.*)

CHEDDAR. Jesus, I forgot about that too.

LUNCH. This actually makes me think about the whole thing differently now.

PEPPER. *Yeah. I know.*

CHEDDAR. Are you still paying that off?

PEPPER. Uh, yessss. That's why I asked to cover your Saturday shifts.

CHEDDAR. *Damn.*

GEMMA. You guys?

PEPPER. Do you know how much it costs to have an ambulance come if you say, have no insurance, and B, you were totally wrong and no one even needed an ambulance?

GEMMA. No idea.

PEPPER. A ton of money Gemma.

Just. A ton of it.

CHEDDAR. *Lots.*

GEMMA. Give me the phone.

LUNCH. We're not paying for this.

CHEDDAR. No way.

PEPPER. All I'm saying Gemma is that it's *lots* and if Rex isn't in need of it? Well, that worries me.

CHEDDAR. She can't afford to be financially responsible.

GEMMA. You wouldn't be.

>*(PEPPER snorts.)*

PEPPER. Well.

LUNCH. I wish there was some way to be sure.

>*(CHEDDAR elbows LUNCH with a snort.)*

CHEDDAR. Imagine if Peps now had *two* ambulance bills to pay.

>*(They all chortle.)*

GEMMA. I don't think we're in a position to make that call.

>*(Beat.)*

PEPPER. Okay. Then we're on the same page. No call.

GEMMA. That's not / what I said.

LUNCH. You said to not make the call.

GEMMA. No, I said it's not *us* that can make the call whether making the call is the right call. *Lunch-bag.*

PEPPER. *(Only I call him Lunch-bag.)* Hey.

LUNCH. Ohh, didn't follow the logic there.

CHEDDAR. I think I'm with Gemma now, we should call.

PEPPER. Then it's your responsibility.

LUNCH. Make her like sign her name on a rock or something, a contract.

PEPPER. No, that's dumb.

LUNCH. Oh.

CHEDDAR. Fine. Gemma, call.

PEPPER. What do you bet / I'm sure he's totally curled up.

GEMMA. I'm not supposed to bet anymore.

LUNCH. He did have that big sweatshirt.

CHEDDAR. Yeah, like that weird Ritz Carlton sweatshirt.

PEPPER. *The.* The Ritz Carlton sweatshirt.

He loves that thing.

There's always a "The" in front of "Ritz."

GEMMA. That's dumb.

CHEDDAR. He loved that thing.

(**PEPPER** *tosses the burner to* **GEMMA.**)

(**GEMMA** *flips it open and calls* **911.**)

911. 9-1-1, how can I help you?

GEMMA. We're out near the Yakima River Basin,
by the rocks that are probably,
we bet,
only *one* million years old.
Our Store Manager and Troop Marshall – Rex –

LUNCH.	CHEDDAR.	PEPPER.
Say his full name.	Rex Jeremy Johnson the Third.	Do the whole thing.

GEMMA. His formal name is Rex Jeremy Johnson the Third?
Has been pulled into an old cave by a huge bear.

(*If this play was a PowerPoint presentation, there would be a fast wipe to the left dissolve to the next scene with a gust of wind like sound for accompaniment. Woosh.*)

***

(*Later.*)

(**GEMMA**'s *been finding little things on the ground then rubbing them together, trying to spark a Signal Fire.*)

CHEDDAR. What are you even doing?

GEMMA. I'm starting a Signal Fire.

CHEDDAR. Oh. It looks like you're just rubbing little things together.

GEMMA. That's *how you make fire.*
Everyone start rubbing things together!

(*No one does.*)

*(**LUNCH** dumps the rest of the contents of **REX**'s bag out.)*

LUNCH. A pack of gum,
    Neti Pot,
    string,
    Duct tape,
    little mirror,
    weird book,
    weird journal,
    small flashlight,
    fifty dollar bill,
    and shoelaces.

*(**PEPPER** tucks the fifty in her shirt.)*

It's occurring to me we are not very equipped.

PEPPER. I mean, I was hoping for a Tranq Gun.

CHEDDAR. You sound ridiculous saying that.

PEPPER. Tranq gun. Tranq gun. Tranq gun.

CHEDDAR. I'm just calling it like I see it.

PEPPER. Tranq gun.

GEMMA. Give me that flashlight.

PEPPER. Don't waste the battery. It's not even dark yet.

GEMMA. I just want to see if it works.

(It does and it's actually really bright for being so small.)

This is actually really bright for being so small.

LUNCH. Oh sweet – a bird book.

*(**LUNCH** picks up the bird book and dives right in.)*

CHEDDAR. I think we should call 9-1-1 again.

LUNCH. I think I spot a Yellow-billed loon.

PEPPER. Einstein, the phone's dead.

CHEDDAR. They said they're coming.

GEMMA. Well, they said to build a Signal Fire.

CHEDDAR. They know how to triangulate the signal or something.

LUNCH. I'm hungry.

>(**LUNCH** *grabs the pack of gum and takes a piece.*)

>(*He throws it back down in the pile of stuff.*)

>(**CHEDDAR** *picks it up and turns to* **PEPPER**.)

CHEDDAR. Do you...

Would you like some gum?

PEPPER. What kind?

CHEDDAR. Oh, I'm not sure.

No packaging.

Lunch?

>(**LUNCH**, *who is already chewing it, doesn't say.*)

LUNCH. Hey, it's just gum man.

>(**CHEDDAR** *is strangely concerned about the packaging, or, rather, lack of packaging.*)

CHEDDAR. The front packaging where...

That sleeve thing? Gone.

>(*Looks closer at the packaging.*)

Ahhhh, see, looks like it was a *double pack* see?

There's a sleeve where the sealed packaging part, where it says the type? But –

>(*Mimes it with his hands how it slides in...it's looks pretty...sexual slash sad. Everyone's a bit confused.*)

– it slides in?

Inside it.

Protects the inside packaging...

Well, it, *it's*, slid...off.

Not sure where it is...so...unclear...on the flavor.

GEMMA & PEPPER.   **CHEDDAR.**

I don't like Cinnamon.   I'm sure it's mint.

LUNCH. It's Cinnamon.

And that's disgusting.

You're...disgusting.

(Does a failed attempt at blowing a bubble.)

Let me know if anyone spots a Black-footed albatross.

(Sounds from the cave.)

(Heavy bear breathing.)

(Labored shuffling.)

PEPPER. *(To* **GEMMA.***)* Did he ever tell you about the hotel?

CHEDDAR. Oh no...

GEMMA. What hotel?

LUNCH. Yeah...

PEPPER. How the first five thousand dollars the Troops raise needs to go to cover that hotel room bill in Nashville?

LUNCH. I *know* about the hotel.

GEMMA. Raise money?

PEPPER. Some people don't know –

LUNCH. *Well I both knew and know.*

PEPPER. I wasn't sure you knew it was *Nashville.* Some people don't know –

LUNCH.   **PEPPER.**

I knew it was Nashville.   – how to behave in hotels apparently.

CHEDDAR. I'm not sure it was Nashville. It could have been Asheville or, even Louisville.

PEPPER. It was Nashville.

Be-*lieve* me.

There used to be a lot of calls from that good ole 6-1-5 area code.

GEMMA. What did he do?

PEPPER. It hardly matters now.

> *(She quick-glances at the cave then picks up his journal.)*

Should we read his journal?

> *(It's a beaten looking little book with the word ORACLE hand written on the front.)*

GEMMA. Are we NOT starting a signal fire?

PEPPER. Ched's right, they'll find us. *Triangulation.*

> *(She opens the journal.)*

Let's learn about Rex.

> *(She opens to a random page and reads.)*

"Roger never would have done that

Roger's off fighting dragons

Roger would not have burned the toast

Roger had such humor, he was the funny one

Roger was so good looking, remember all the girls

Roger never needed to cut his meat, it flew straight to his mouth, bite size from the plate

Roger could've been the king of some small country if he wanted

Oh, Roger is the king of some small country now

PUSH HERE.

> *("Push Here" is written in the book with a circle around it like a button. **PEPPER** pushes it and underscoring music* comes on underscoring the rest of the entry read.)*

Roger changed his name to Samuel.

Samuel's a racecar driver in the South.

The youngest looks like Samuel.

We have named him Roger.

---

* A license to produce *Tin Cat Shoes* does not include a performance license for any third-party or copyrighted recordings. Licensees should create their own.

He was only fifteen when he left
He was twenty when he left
He left when he was twenty-nine
He left when he turned thirty-three
He's been gone since he was seven.

Roger drove the chariot to the sun and back, bringing us flame, showing us light. He left us the light, but took the chariot. He left us a marinade, but took the steak. He took the dining room table, but left us the plates. He left us the plates, but had the forks in his pocket as he drove away. As we watched him all the way up the hill, getting smaller and smaller until all we could see were two wings pushing down with all their might, crushing the air back towards earth as he boomeranged into the stratosphere. The air denser now, a hole in the sky the only clear mark that he had even been here in the first place."

CHEDDAR. Who the hell is Roger?

PEPPER. See, I feel like Rex has a lot of secrets.

LUNCH. Maybe Roger was Rex's brother, I remember something about a brother that was the black sheep. Or, maybe Rex was the black sheep.

GEMMA. I'm the blackship.

LUNCH. The what?

GEMMA. Were you the blackship?

LUNCH. I don't know what you are saying.

GEMMA. Blackship.

LUNCH. Black. Ship?

GEMMA. Blackship.

CHEDDAR. She means like a "pirate" I bet.

PEPPER. Black SHEEP.

GEMMA. Blackship. The odd one.

LUNCH. Not "blackship."

GEMMA. Blackship.

LUNCH. Black. <u>Sheep.</u>

GEMMA. That's what I'm *saying*.

>（**GEMMA** *pulls a scroll out of* **REX**'s *bag.*)

Here's, well, I guess it's a scroll?

PEPPER. Un-scroll it dummy.

GEMMA. *Dummy?*

LUNCH. Maybe it's a deed.

PEPPER. It's *not* a deed.

GEMMA. It's a deed!

PEPPER. How do you know it's a deed?

GEMMA. It says DEED at the top.
Like a weird old land deed.

>*(She shows them the scroll; it says DEED at the top.)*

>*(They all look towards the cave.)*

CHEDDAR. *There's so much about Rex we don't know.*

>***

>*(Some time passes.)*

>*(Everyone is waiting.)*

>（**LUNCH** *is sitting near* **PEPPER.**）

LUNCH. …I used to watch you.
In the employee room.

PEPPER. You're not supposed to tell people that.

LUNCH. No, it's okay.

>*(She's going to ignore him, then doesn't ignore him.)*

PEPPER. Why would you watch me.

LUNCH. Because I had this idea that…
That you never swallowed.
Like your saliva…
And then Cheddar told me that you didn't blink.
And then we had the idea.
We'd convinced ourselves that you were, you know.

PEPPER. No.

LUNCH. Not exactly *human.*

> Then we heard all these other things too.
>
> It's stupid, but from like past employees.

PEPPER. Past employees??

LUNCH. Some of your Whole Foods friends?

PEPPER. Those guys were real *jerks.*

LUNCH. We heard that no one ever picked you up after work,

> but that you lived really far away.
>
> That you never had to go to the bathroom.
>
> That your hair didn't move,
>
> even when you ran.
>
> But no one had ever *seen* you running,
>
> so that one was...rumor.
>
> It seemed like. Then.

PEPPER. Is that all?

LUNCH. Everyone knew you *brought* your lunch to work,

> but no one could confirm you *ate* your lunch.
>
> You seemed to give away a lot of your little snacks,
>
> but you never wanted anything *in return for it.*
>
> Certain people,
>
> it's kinda weird to say,
>
> but certain people,
>
> wondered about your...
>
> "Intentions."

> > *(Beat.)*

PEPPER. I think I need to be alone for a little while.

> *(**PEPPER** turns her back to the group.)*

> *(**LUNCH** casually migrates back to the others. He kicks the ground.)*

LUNCH. Look at how much dirt is everywhere.

> The weeds? *God.*

The shards of rocks?

What are those, _boulders_?

GEMMA. Lunch, we're outside.

LUNCH. Is anyone going to clean this up?

CHEDDAR. This is what outside _is_.

GEMMA. Clean what / up?

LUNCH. Well, it's a mess.

CHEDDAR. It's not a mess, this is natural.

GEMMA. You know, _nature_.

LUNCH. They could keep it a little tidier.

CHEDDAR. They?

LUNCH. It's not even organized. They should keep things together.

GEMMA.	**CHEDDAR**.
Like...shoes?	It's not someone's job to rake and organize _nature_.

LUNCH. By the look of things, I'm not surprised to hear that.

CHEDDAR. Haven't you been outside before?

LUNCH. What about those _Rangers_.

CHEDDAR. Hey Lunch. _Earth to LUNCH- / bag_. The Rangers make sure you don't light a coke can or some chip bag on fire.

LUNCH. Don't call me Lunch-bag you know I hate that.

> (**GEMMA** _sniffles, but not from crying, just from like allergies._)

> (**CHEDDAR** _hands her the Neti Pot._)

What, do you have a cold now?

GEMMA. No, allergies.

> (**PEPPER** _has wandered back to them._)

PEPPER. Did you just call her an old cow?

> (_Beat._)

LUNCH. No?

CHEDDAR. Maybe you should Neti Pot.

GEMMA. Maybe you should kill yourself.

CHEDDAR. Neti Potting is the most ancient and pure way to help relieve your symptoms. *Gemma.*

> *(They are quiet.)*
>
> *(It's gotten darker, and colder.)*
>
> (**LUNCH** *kicks some dirt and lets out a small, involuntary yelp.*)
>
> (**CHEDDAR** *slips off his shoes. He paces around deciding where to set them.*)
>
> *(He sets them in the middle.)*

PEPPER. No.

CHEDDAR. Come on!

What else are we doing.

> (**GEMMA** *gets the flashlight and puts it on top of a little rock pile then turns it on.*)

GEMMA. Signal Fire...

> (**LUNCH** *sighs and takes his shoes off, tossing them in with* **CHEDDAR**'s.)

CHEDDAR. One game. The loser goes for help.

GEMMA. What game.

LUNCH. Oh, it's so great.

Shoe Sort.

Take your shoes off,

throw them in the pile.

We mix them up and form a circle facing away from the shoes.

Then, on somebody's "GO" –

PEPPER & CHEDDAR. GO!

LUNCH. – we turn and the first person that gets their shoes on wins.

GEMMA. Uh… *Shoe sort?*

PEPPER. Alright.

> (**PEPPER** *throws her shoes on the pile.*)

I'm in.

> (*A soft glow appears over a mountain.*)

Look! There's a light over there, behind the mountain.

LUNCH. Okay, last person to get their shoes on seeks help.

GEMMA. Do you guys have any sense of time or space?
That could be miles away?

CHEDDAR. I'm not sure 9-1-1 is coming…

LUNCH. Also, doesn't it feel right? Here we are and then, the glow. Just over there.

GEMMA. We should wait here…

PEPPER. You're a little bit of a dreamer – aren't you Gemma?

CHEDDAR. It feels like we need to up the ante –

GEMMA. Double down?

CHEDDAR. Rex would have liked us to double our efforts.

LUNCH. He was big on doubling efforts.

> (**GEMMA** *takes her shoes off and throws them on the pile.*)
>
> (*She has a really big hole in one of her socks, her toes stick through.*)
>
> (*Everyone decides not to judge her.*)
>
> (**LUNCH** *mixes the shoes up haphazardly like a Caesar Salad.*)

TIN CAT TROOPS! Please form a circle around the shoes.

> (*They do.*)

Everyone take a giant step out.

> (*They do.*)

On my Go –

PEPPER. Nope, on MY "Go."

LUNCH. Fine, on Pep's "Go."

PEPPER. GO.

> *(The Shoe Sort is on!)*
>
> *(All of them are lunging, twisting, turning, crawling, slithering, over, under, on top of each other. Shoes are found, shoes are thrown (what is this, croquet?), shoes are hid. It is wild and fierce.)*
>
> *(It is both a pounding ballet and vibrant dance of bodies under moving disco conditions. A selfish orgy of survival but also a brutal, quite beautiful, burlesque...)*
>
> *(GEMMA and CHEDDAR are rolling around on the ground tearing at little parts of each other. GEMMA is dominant but CHED is a little quicker, he can't move at all as her back foot finds its way into her right shoe.)*
>
> *(PEPPER is trying to pull LUNCH's arms off, then is distracted by the sight of one of her shoes and rolls over to it.)*
>
> *(CHEDDAR sits, crying to himself, gathering the shoes one by one and tossing them around again. The mission of the game seems to have alluded him. He pulls his shirt up, over his head, and goes fetal.)*
>
> *(LUNCH falls hard, twisting his ankle.)*
>
> *(The glow behind the distant mountain increases, brighter and brighter until they're all staring at it, entranced by the beauty and the unspoken promise of new adventure.)*
>
> *(GEMMA crawls to the crevice that REX was pulled into and whispers through the crack to the bear...)*

***

GEMMA. Do you know the song?

    The one about the bear?

BEAR VOICE. Where the bear mauls the Troop leader?

GEMMA. It's a call and repeat song-type-thing.

BEAR VOICE. No.

GEMMA. It's dumb.

    It's from camp.

    Goes like this:

    The other day

BEAR VOICE. The other day

GEMMA. *I met a bear*

BEAR VOICE. I met a bear

GEMMA. *In tennis shoes*

BEAR VOICE. In tennis shoes

GEMMA. *And underwear*

BEAR VOICE. And underwear

GEMMA & BEAR VOICE. *The other day I met a bear,*

    in tennis shoes and underwear.

GEMMA. *He looked at me*

BEAR VOICE. He looked at me

GEMMA. *I looked at him*

BEAR VOICE. I looked at him

GEMMA. *He sized me up*

BEAR VOICE. He sized me up

GEMMA. *I sized up him*

BEAR VOICE. I sized up him

GEMMA, BEAR VOICE & ALL. *He looked at me I looked at him,*

    he sized me up I sized up him.

GEMMA. *He said to me*

BEAR VOICE. He said to me

GEMMA. *Why don't you run...*

BEAR VOICE. Why don't you run –

    Why don't you run –

    Why don't you run –

(**GEMMA** *backs away from the crevice, with growing inspiration...*)

GEMMA. ...There's more.

BEAR VOICE. Why don't you run –

GEMMA. I can't remember exactly how it ends...

BEAR VOICE. Why don't you run –

GEMMA. *(To* **PEPPER** *and* **LUNCH** *and* **CHEDDAR**.*)*
   You guys... The *mountain*. The *light*.
   Something's yonder over there.
   It has to be.
   Behind that mountain.
   Fuck the Signal Fire.
   Fuck *Triangulation*.
   Let's Triple Cat down.
   Let's Tin Cat Troop this.
   Who's with me? Huh? Who's with me???

      (**LUNCH** *holds his injured ankle; he's been unable to get up.*)

LUNCH. One of us should stay here.

PEPPER. No, we need to stick together.

GEMMA. We can make it.

LUNCH. I –
   I twisted my ankle –

CHEDDAR. I'll stay with –

LUNCH. *NO.* I'll be fine.

CHEDDAR. I don't want to leave you.

LUNCH. I know, but –
   I'll be the one that stays.

CHEDDAR. What do you mean?

GEMMA. Lunch, we can find you a crutch.

CHEDDAR. Yeah, like a stick or –

PEPPER. An old sword or something!

LUNCH. It's just easier if you...guys go.

(Beat.)

(Beat.)

(Beat.)

CHEDDAR. ...Lunch...

PEPPER. The good news? This isn't *Mount Everest*. We're not leaving you on the side of the mountain to freeze and be found in ten years when they're shooting an M&M commercial.

LUNCH. Also, it's like sixty-five degrees out.

GEMMA. Lunch, are you sure?

LUNCH. Besides, I'm really into the bird book.

CHEDDAR. But Lunch...

LUNCH. I'll be looking for a male Western Tanager!

GEMMA. We should go before it gets darker.

LUNCH. They have this really cute splash of red on their head.

CHEDDAR. There's so much...

LUNCH. Hey, I'm not going anywhere.

PEPPER. Leave him the burner.

> *(GEMMA flips him the burner phone.)*

LUNCH. I appreciate the gesture, but there's nowhere to charge it.

CHEDDAR. I don't like this –

LUNCH. Ched, I'm fine. Go.

CHEDDAR. I'm feeling...

Very *upset*.

LUNCH. Go, get out there.

> *(PEPPER flips LUNCH a Kind Bar.)*

PEPPER. For later.

LUNCH. Thanks, Pep-Squad.

GEMMA. Alright.

CHEDDAR. I want to say something so stupid.

LUNCH. Ched, you couldn't say anything stupid.

CHEDDAR. I love you.

>   (**LUNCH** *smiles for a little too long.*)

LUNCH. I love you too.

PEPPER. Shut up you guys.

>   Lunch, see you in an hour.

GEMMA. *Tops.*

LUNCH. The funniest part? You guys look like such a good team right now. Rex would love it.

GEMMA. Lunch... Shoe sort was really both weird and fun. I'm sorry you got injured.

PEPPER. Chin up Lunch-bag.

CHEDDAR. Later skater.

LUNCH. After 'while croc-face.

>   (**LUNCH** *opens the bird book and leans back against the cave.*)

>   (*The others leave towards the glowing light, quietly singing as an eagle soars overhead.*)

[MUSIC: "TIN CAT TROOP SONG"]

ALL.

>   WE ARE THE TIN CAT TROOPS
>   PACK 3-4-2-7-1
>   WE'RE LOYAL TO OUR FRIENDS AND DEN
>   UP TO THE VERY, VERY END, END, END...

THE UPS CALL INTERLUDE

(Far away, the phone (landline) rings at a deserted Tin Cat Shoes.)

(The answering machine eventually picks up, it's **REX***'s voice.)*

TIN CAT SHOES PHONE MESSAGE. Bonjour!
You've reached Tin Cat Shoes!
Even though we're not here
Christmas is our favorite time of year!
So, if shoe presents are what you're looking for
congratulations, you've called the right store!
(PEPPER, LUNCH, CHEDDAR:) Leave a message!

ROGER, THE UPS DELIVERY PERSON'S VOICEMAIL. Tin Cat
Kittens!
It's me, Roger, your friendly UPS delivery person.
Come on, where is everyone? Vacation?
I'm out front and I've got forty-three boxes to deliver
post-mark from –

(Checking.)

– the Nordic Countries.
Stamped Urgent.
But...you're not here.
I guess I'll wait? I don't mind, last stop...
Nothing really going on at home...
plus, I'll sit and eat my chips!

(Chomp, chomp.)

They're delicious.

PART THREE: THE CASINO

(The Casino is a cacophony of lights, sparkle, chance, survival, and money.)

*(**GEMMA** dabs at the light sweat forming on her upper lip.)*

*(**PEPPER** wipes her palms on her arms as she surveys the room.)*

*(Chunks of laughter escape a wide-eyed **CHEDDAR**.)*

*(**THE CROUPIER** presides over the Roulette table and there's more than a bit of a resemblance to **REX**.)*

(Note: If possible all air conditioners should be on at full blast so the room gets as cold as possible as fast as possible.)

GEMMA. Stay close, and stick with me.

PEPPER. I'm in.

*(**PEPPER** throws a fifty on the table.)*

THE CROUPIER. What's a fifty, right?

PEPPER. *Stupid fifty.*

THE CROUPIER. You can't put a price on *dreams*!

*(**THE CROUPIER** slides **PEPPER** a stack of chips.)*

CHEDDAR. I'm gonna to do a lap around this place, check it out.

*(**CHEDDAR** takes off jogging.)*

THE CROUPIER. You can't put a price on *experience.*

PEPPER. Gemma, you in?

GEMMA. I don't carry as much *cash* as, as I used to.

THE CROUPIER. You'll find cash machines to the right, and to the left.
Up a level, and in the bathrooms.

GEMMA. Cash is best kept pressed against your skin.

THE CROUPIER. Hey – like I always say? You can't put a price on *chance*.

GEMMA. It's safer to have your money *on your body*.

And against your skin is safest.

(**CHEDDAR** *returns from his jog.*)

CHEDDAR. Holy *Fortress of Existence*, this place is HUGE.

Sick views from the back porch. Killer race track.

Man, WHERE'S THE WAITRESS? I need a drink STAT.

Jesus. Guys, I think I saw my high school econ teacher, ole *Father Hamlen*, playing five bucks a spin on a Wheel of Fortune Game.

GEMMA. Father Hamlen from High School?

CHEDDAR. Father Hamlen / from High School!

GEMMA. Oh / no...

PEPPER. *(Singing.)*

"MY FRONT RUNNER IS VALENTINE –"

GEMMA. How much does Father Hamlen make?

CHEDDAR. Hell, thirty-five grand a year?

GEMMA. Okay. He's either really stupid or really smart, because, by my calculations, if he's playing five bucks a spin he's only got about seven thousand spins before his entire paycheck is spent.

CHEDDAR. Seems like a lot of spins.

PEPPER. I'm sure he won't lose every single time.

(**THE CROUPIER** *chuckles and* **GEMMA** *and he exchange a knowing look. Ha!*)

GEMMA. Really? Are you sure? Because people DO loose every single time, Pepper.

It just amps them up, just gets them going.

It's a high you couldn't begin to know.

THE CROUPIER. Hey, looks like we got a ringer here!

GEMMA. Mr. Croupier –

THE CROUPIER. Just Croupier is fine –

GEMMA. Croupier, I'm going to come out and say it – you bear –

PEPPER. Ha!

GEMMA. Ha! You bear more than a resemblance to our fearless shoe store manager and troop leader who has been sucked –

PEPPER. Possibly pulled –

GEMMA. Sucked or pulled into a cave BY a bear.

Do you happen to know or have any relation to a Mr. Rex Jeremy Johnson the Third?

THE CROUPIER. Let me share a bit of knowledge: if you look hard enough for something – you find something. Even if that something isn't the something you originally thought you were looking for. It's a different something. But... Looks now, now that it's in front of you and now that you've been searching so long, so very long, it now looks just like that original something.

PEPPER. I think he's onto something.

GEMMA. May we use your phone?

THE CROUPIER. Bets?

> (**GEMMA** *is unsure if* **THE CROUPIER** *has meant this as a challenge, she moves closer to the Roulette table.*)

CHEDDAR. Someone stake me – I don't have my wallet.

GEMMA. Cheddar, listen to me. *Slippery slope.* If Father Hamlen has a quick wrist? If his machine is new? Hell, he could spin six times *in sixty seconds.* That's thirty bucks a minute. A year of work, of life, distilled to nineteen hours and forty-four minutes sitting on a stool, his lungs full of hyper-pumped-in-fuck-me-I'm-on-top-of-the-world-oxygen. And trust me when I say – he *has never felt more alive.*

THE CROUPIER. It's like a religion.

GEMMA. It *is* like a religion. He's operating on a faith that feeds his most primal instincts.

(God, **GEMMA** *loves Casinos! She searches for*
saliva in her mouth and doesn't find much.)

Fuck! I'm thirsty. Is there any / water?

THE CROUPIER. Last bets!

CHEDDAR. Gem-dawg, just lend me a twenty.

GEMMA. If I lend you any money at all, understand that
I get a thirty percent stake in ALL of your winnings
and you'll pay me back plus twenty-five percent
interest.

PEPPER. Damn.

CHEDDAR. Deal.

*(***GEMMA*** tosses a twenty on the table.)*

*(***THE CROUPIER*** slides* **CHEDDAR** *some chips.)*

GEMMA. *Cheddar...*

CHEDDAR. Gem-dawg.

GEMMA. I'm looking for the highest return.

THE CROUPIER. Smart.

GEMMA. If we're doing this?
  We're doing this.

PEPPER. Guys, this is all very *Casablanca.*

CHEDDAR. Ha! You're right.
  Very "Black 22."

THE CROUPIER. HA! "Black 22!"

PEPPER. Very – you should let it ride on "Black 22."

CHEDDAR. Last call, very "last call!"

THE CROUPIER. Last bets!

CHEDDAR. Very "last bets –"

PEPPER. VERY, "Hey buddy, put it on black 22."

GEMMA. Signs are signs, Cheddar – put it all on Black 22.

CHEDDAR. Let's do it.

GEMMA. Tips are tips and movies are movies –
  but Humphrey Bogart man, I'm always like, "do I trust
  him?"

CHEDDAR & GEMMA. He does own the casino.

> *(Ha! They exchange dazzling looks!)*

Stop it ☺

> *(Eye-locked, they hesitate for only a moment then:)*

JINX!

THE CROUPIER. Everyone's on a journey!

GEMMA. We're just doing the best we can, right?

THE CROUPIER. Everyone's hiding from someone.

PEPPER. You can say that again.

GEMMA. Everyone's just trying to get home.

PEPPER. For sure, everyone's got a *story*.

CHEDDAR. Lunch is gonnnnnnna FREAK.

THE CROUPIER. Lunch? Might I recommend the Nachos.

PEPPER. I've been DYING for some Nachos. See, it's complicated –

GEMMA. What's complicated?

PEPPER. Croupier –

THE CROUPIER. Croup.

PEPPER. Croup, I'm a writer. A *novelist*. My first book? Set at a Whole Foods during the storm of the century.

THE CROUPIER. Dangerously witty.

PEPPER. It's been published in two languages because Braille's a language, right?

CHEDDAR. Your book's in Braille?

PEPPER. Yeah, all kinds of Braille.

GEMMA. Isn't there only one kind of Braille?

PEPPER. Who are you, *Helen Keller*?

GEMMA. What??

> *Eyes* on the *prize*, troops.
> Black 22 seems right. Even in the movie, he's just trying to get "*Get Home*" –

PEPPER. And hey, not everyone even *has* a home...

GEMMA. – and you can't fault him for that.

PEPPER. ...during certain times in their life, I bet.

THE CROUPIER. Everyone has a home / here.

CHEDDAR. I oddly feel at home. Father Hamlen and / all.

>   (**PEPPER** *takes a deep breath.*)

PEPPER. *I feel so alert!*

>   (**GEMMA** *smirks.*)

GEMMA. I wish I had a feather in my hair.

>   (**THE CROUPIER** *spins the Roulette Wheel –.*)

THE CROUPIER. <u>Last bets!</u>

>   (*They've put it all on Black 22.*)

>   (**PEPPER** *runs her hand through her hair.*)

>   (**CHEDDAR** *puts his hands together, closes his eyes, and looks up.*)

>   (**GEMMA** *covers her mouth with a fist.*)

>   (*The ball stops on Black 22.*)

Black 22!

>   (*They all win! They celebrate, they have won a tremendous amount of money. No one has felt emotion like this. They are stunned, they are happy. Chips everywhere!*)

CHEDDAR. Gotta go check on Father Hamlen.

>   (**CHEDDAR** *jogs off.*)

GEMMA. Hey Croup –

You're not, say, a "Systems Guy" are you?

THE CROUPIER. Are you looking for a Systems Guy?

GEMMA. I'm just thinking that if you are, you might not like where I'm going with this –

THE CROUPIER. I have some theories,

some of them are about systems,

but one of my theories is never to label anything,

so, I'd never say I was a Systems Guy,

because it goes against my theories.

GEMMA. You don't... Come from a long line of wartime fabric weavers by any chance?

PEPPER. Gemma!

THE CROUPIER. If only!

GEMMA. Do you?

PEPPER. Don't Grill-dawg the guy – Croup's our lucky charm!

> (**CHEDDAR** *enters wearing a fedora and holding a menu.*)

CHEDDAR. You wouldn't believe this gift shop! The sheer variety of product is *sick*.

Cigars

Sunglasses

All the gum types

And, yep – fedoras.

You like it?

Pep – the Nacho menu.

PEPPER. Boom!

GEMMA. This is serious. What did you all do right before the ball landed on Black 22?

> (**PEPPER** *and* **CHEDDAR** *have no idea what* **GEMMA** *means.*)

What were you doing physically, thinking, saying?

THE CROUPIER. *(To* **GEMMA.***)* Ha, didn't peg you for being one of them.

GEMMA. Think... This is important.

Right before our shiny little ball landed on the glorious Black 22, what happened?

Pepper – I believe you...ran your hand through your hair?

PEPPER. You're right.

GEMMA. And Cheddar – you put your hands together, closed your eyes, and looked up.

CHEDDAR. I did!

GEMMA. I covered my mouth with my fist.

THE CROUPIER. Here we go –

> (**THE CROUPIER** *spins the Roulette Wheel and we hear the little metal ball dropping and going round and round.*)

GEMMA. Exactly the same this time...
We'll let it ride, right?

THE CROUPIER. <u>Last Bets!</u>

CHEDDAR & PEPPER. Let it ride.

GEMMA. Let it ride.

> (*They've let it ride on Black 22.*)

> (**PEPPER** *runs her hand through her hair.*)

> (**CHEDDAR** *puts his hands together, closes his eyes, and looks up.*)

> (**GEMMA** *covers her mouth with a fist.*)

> (*The ball stops on Black 22.*)

THE CROUPIER. Black 22!

> (*They all win! They celebrate, they have won a tremendous amount of money. No one has felt emotion like this. They are stunned, they are happy. Chips everywhere!*)

> (**THE CROUPIER** *is counting out their winnings and sliding each huge stacks of chips.*)

> (**PEPPER**'s *still clutching the Nacho menu.*)

PEPPER. Who do I see about these Nachos?

THE CROUPIER. Who do you *want* to see about them, right?

PEPPER. You're a real sage, Croup.

> (**THE CROUPIER** *gives* **PEPPER** *a slinky wink.*)

THE CROUPIER. Eh, just your typical gatekeeper of dreams.

GEMMA. Charmer of snakes –

THE CROUPIER. If this keeps up, we're going to run out of chips!

PEPPER. How much money do you think we have?

GEMMA. Don't think about it like that –

THE CROUPIER. Let's just say you've made the best $70 investment you'll ever make.

PEPPER. What's an example of something we could afford to buy now?

GEMMA. A house in Madison, Wisconsin.

PEPPER.   **CHEDDAR.**

  Magic.   Ew.

GEMMA.

  A smallish Yacht.   Better.

PEPPER. My thoughts are racing.

GEMMA. Around five thousand plates of Nachos.

PEPPER. Nachos. Croup, you might not be interested in hearing about the writer's block I've had after
Storm Foods, but let me tell you it's like it's <u>lifted</u>. Novel numero dos? Is about Fucking Nachos.

CHEDDAR. That's fucking genius, Pep.

PEPPER. Chicken. Fucking. Nachos.

CHEDDAR. Everyone. Loves. Nachos.

THE CROUPIER. And, to my knowledge, no one's ever written a great Nacho Novel before.

PEPPER. Black beans. Sides of guac.

THE CROUPIER. You're onto something.

PEPPER. Melted cheese. *Asparagus tips*.

GEMMA. Your toppings are a little all over the place.

THE CROUPIER. Your little troop group is dripping with good fortune.

  I've been hoping to meet some people like you...

    (Leans in.)

  How much do you guys know about –

    (Paranoid looks over both shoulders.)

  Forget it.

  <u>Last bets!</u>

GEMMA. Talk about what –

PEPPER. Should we...

GEMMA. Know about what –

PEPPER. Cash out?

GEMMA. *Let it ride.*

CHEDDAR. Let it ride!

PEPPER. Let it Ride!

> (**PEPPER** *thinks about how endlessly amazing her Nacho Novel will be.*)

Grilled hamburger...iceberg lettuce...*sour cream*!

GEMMA. You realize you're just naming ingredients, right?

PEPPER. *This thing's gonna practically write itself.*

THE CROUPIER. You know who else just named ingredients? Shakespeare.

PEPPER. Thank you!

THE CROUPIER. I'd read your Nacho Novel.

CHEDDAR. Me too.

> (**GEMMA** *says nothing.*)

PEPPER. Gemma, I'd of thought you of all people would understand?

GEMMA. Why?

PEPPER. Unlike the others, you seem*ed* to have goals.

GEMMA. I met you this morning?

> (*The little metal ball drops and goes round and round.*)

THE CROUPIER. Last bets!

> (**PEPPER** *stares deep into* **GEMMA**'s *eyes.*)

PEPPER. Tomatillos? Diced tomatoes? Roasted *corn*? Onions, Pico de G*allo*, *Jalapeño slices.*

Does that *just sound* like ingredients, Gemma?

GEMMA. Yes.

THE CROUPIER. Last bets!

GEMMA, PEPPER & CHEDDAR. Let it ride!

(They've let it ride on Black 22.)

(**PEPPER** *runs her hand through her hair.*)

(**CHEDDAR** *puts his hands together, closes his eyes, and looks up.*)

(**GEMMA** *covers her mouth with a fist.*)

(The ball stops on Black 22.)

THE CROUPIER. Black 22!

(They all win. They celebrate, they have won a tremendous amount of money. No one has felt emotion like this. They are stunned, they are happy. Chips everywhere!)

CHEDDAR. YOU GUYS:

(**CHEDDAR** *does that thing where he balances a small stack of chips on his elbow then brings his hand and forearm forward with warp speed – catching the entire stack in his hand. Everyone claps! He's brilliant!*)

(**DANNY** *appears – he looks more than a little like* **LUNCH**, *but different.*)

THE CROUPIER. Troops, this is Danny.
Danny's your Dedicated Nacho Waiter.
Danny's job is to talk, to really, truly talk to you about *what you want on your nachos.*

(Beat.)

PEPPER. Danny. I've been waiting for you my entire life.

(Introductions.)

Pepper. Gemma. Cheddar.

(**DANNY** *salutes them.*)

CHEDDAR. At ease, friend!

(**GEMMA** *raises her hand slightly.*)

GEMMA. Dairy allergy.
Friend.

THE CROUPIER. Unlike other waiters, Danny has nothing but *time* and serves no one but *you.*

His knowledge is both deep and diverse and he has zero problem with people who can't make up their mind. It's a specialty of his. He's worked miracles, made the pickiest of eaters happy, kept the most doubtful of doubters satisfied, but perhaps the one quality that makes him outstanding is that Danny *LOVES HIS JOB.*

DANNY. I'm not even bothered by the occasional sogginess of a tortilla chip.

THE CROUPIER. Right, Danny?

DANNY. Personally? They're the pearl of the plate.

THE CROUPIER. Tell them the part about the tomatoes.

DANNY. Deep in the hills of Italy, there is a field with soil so sweet you can eat it. It's here our cherished Roma Tomatoes have grown for five centuries.

> *(Big smile.)*

Our Nachos...are available with these tomatoes.

THE CROUPIER. Tell them about how we cut the jalapeños.

DANNY. Our blades are sharpened by hand with diamonds in the hills outside PyeongChang. These same blades are wrapped many times with soft sleeves woven with the feathers of the Red-crowned crane to keep them safe on their journey to our Casino.

THE CROUPIER. The process of roasting the cauliflower.

DANNY. At six hundred degrees for seven minutes, with a dash of salt and olive oil.

(To **GEMMA**.*)* We crumble it small so it looks akin to feta cheese, but, of course, it is only cauliflower. So, dairy free.

GEMMA. That sounds very good.

CHEDDAR. Guys – order whatever, I'm easy.

I'll be right back!

> *(***CHEDDAR** *jogs off.)*

PEPPER. Danny, quick interview, as the only Nacho waiter I've ever met, tell me – what's your secret?

DANNY. Croup. He taught me everything I know, the secret is – as they say – in the cheese sauce.

THE CROUPIER. Danny studied for a long time, he worked hard to be the person he is today. Like with anything, Danny's made the sacrifices.

DANNY. But, with pleasure.

PEPPER. Danny, I think I'm ready to have a serious conversation about toppings.

(**CHEDDAR** *jogs back in, looking more and more* Guys and Dolls, *he's holding a Racing Form.*)

CHEDDAR. Gemma's-on-Fire! Gemma's-on-Fire!

GEMMA. What??

CHEDDAR. Father Hamlen says she's a long shot, but her morning workout looked good and she likes a sloppy track – so, his money's on her! The race is about to start.

(**GEMMA** *slides* **CHEDDAR** *a stack of chips.*)

GEMMA. Put it all on Gemma's-on-Fire to win. Go!

(**CHEDDAR** *takes jogs off.*)

PEPPER. Danny, what are your thoughts on black olives?

DANNY. Nutritionally? Chocked full of antioxidants, tons of healthy fat. But personally? I'm a *Kalamata* guy. You just need to know *where you stand.*

THE CROUPIER. LAST BETS!

GEMMA. We stand with Black 22.

(**CHEDDAR** *jogs back on.*)

CHEDDAR. Father Hamlen's placing our bet. Frankly, I'm worried about him... He's not really taking to retirement, his wife is ill, his dog has died.

GEMMA. I'm thinking we should have bet the Trifecta.

CHEDDAR. It's a small race, seven horses: Gemma's-on-Fire, LongWayHome, Jason-Jacuzzi-Bad-Idea, Lucky Peaches, Epitaph, Valentine and Paul Revere.

(**GEMMA** *takes the Racing Form from* **CHEDDAR.**)

GEMMA. Who has a pencil?

> *(The little metal ball drops and goes round and round.)*

DANNY. I do!

> *(**DANNY** hands **GEMMA** the pencil from behind his ear.)*

> *(**GEMMA** starts taking notes on the Racing Form, analyzing the stats.)*

GEMMA. Let's put Gemma's-on-Fire on top with Lucky Peaches and LongWayHome boxed underneath.

CHEDDAR. Boxed?

GEMMA. *Just tell him that.*

THE CROUPIER. Last bets!

> *(This all happens like before, but much faster now.)*

> *(**PEPPER** runs her hand through her hair.)*

> *(**CHEDDAR** puts his hands together, closes his eyes, and looks up.)*

> *(**GEMMA** covers her mouth with a fist.)*

Black 22!

> *(They all win!)*

Croyez-vous que tout mène à quelque chose?

> *(They celebrate!)*

GEMMA. Quoi? Tu parles français? Je parle français, moi!

> *(They have won a tremendous amount of money!)*

THE CROUPIER. Oui oui?

> *(No one has felt emotion like this!)*

GEMMA. Oui! Oui!

> *(They are happy!)*

> *(**CHEDDAR** happily starts jogging off –.)*

GEMMA. Ched! *Arrête!*

    (**CHEDDAR** *stops.*)

I changed my mind.

Let's do a couple exacta boxes.

THE CROUPIER. J'aime le feu dans votre esprit!

GEMMA. Gemma's-on-Fire and Epitaph.

And Paul Revere with Jason-Jacuzzi-Bad-Idea.

Get more chips.

    (**CHEDDAR** *goes back to the table and scoops a stack of chips into his shirt.*)

    (*He starts off again…*)

Wait!

THE CROUPIER. Danny – tell them about the Nacho Club.

DANNY. Pepper, so, we have a Nacho Club.

If you sign up, and if you show up, ten free toppings.

PEPPER. Damn.

DANNY.

I know. No restrictions either.

    (**CHEDDAR** *stops as* **GEMMA** *consults the form hard.*)

PEPPER.

Is it extra for bacon?

GEMMA.

Let's box that first Tri.

DANNY.

Nope. We believe in customer service *and* loyalty.

CHEDDAR.

Okay –

PEPPER.

Hey, our shoe store believed in that!

THE CROUPIER.

Customer service is the key to enlightenment, right Danny?

GEMMA.

And, bet *LongWayHome* to win, place and show.

DANNY.

Infinity times right. Pep, when you worked at the shoe store –

CHEDDAR.

Okay –

PEPPER.

Tin Cat Shoes –

DANNY.

When you worked at Tin Cat Shoes, did you ever just bash your head into the wall?

PEPPER.

No, ha!

GEMMA.

Put a thousand to win on Valentine.

DANNY.

Like, boom!

PEPPER.

That would hurt.

CHEDDAR.

(To GEMMA.*)* Hey, your nose is bleeding.

*(*GEMMA*'s nose is bleeding, she is consumed with the race form and barely notices.)*

*(*PEPPER *starts humming the "Tin Cat Troop Song.")*

THE CROUPIER.

Gemma.

GEMMA.

PEPPER.

We did sing a lot though.

Shit, have him do one with Jason-Jacuzzi-Bad-Idea, Epitaph and LongWayHome –

DANNY.

Teach me.

> (**CHEDDAR** *is unsure*
> *if she's done figuring*
> *out the bet or not)*

THE CROUPIER.

Hey, Gemma.

GEMMA.

Ugh, and...

> (**THE CROUPIER** *holds the*
> *little Roulette ball up.)*

PEPPER.

Repeat after me.

[MUSIC: "TIN CAT TROOP SONG"]

WE ARE THE TIN CAT
TROOPS –

> (**CHEDDAR** *is unsure if*
> *she's done or not.)*

GEMMA.

Let's do a Trifecta Wheel.
Put Lucky Peaches on
top, with the rest boxed
underneath.

CHEDDAR.

Okay!
Should I go?

DANNY.

WE ARE THE TIN CAT
TROOPS –

GEMMA.

Wait –

PEPPER.

PACK 3-4-2-7-1 –

THE CROUPIER.

Gemm-ma-ma-ma.

DANNY.
> PACK 3-4-2-7-1 –
>> *(A slight shift.)*

NARRATOR.
> AND SO,
> OUR STORY NOW
> COMES TO AN END...

>> (**GEMMA** *consults the form* <u>*hard.*</u>)

PEPPER.
> WE'RE LOYAL TO OUR
>> FRIENDS AND DEN –

DANNY.
> WE'RE LOYAL TO OUR
>> FRIENDS AND DEN –

CHEDDAR.
Should I go now?

GEMMA.
One sec –

NARRATOR.
> NEEDLESS TO SAY –

>> (**GEMMA** *consults the form hard.*)

PEPPER & DANNY.
> UP TO THE VERY, VERY END! END! END!

NARRATOR. WHEN THE AERO NORDIC BOOT ARRIVED AT TIN CAT SHOES THAT DAY, NO ONE WAS THERE TO RECEIVE THE SHIPMENT.

PEPPER. You're a natural!

DANNY. Hey –

> *(Reaches his hand out for* **PEPPER***'s.)*

There's something special I want to show you. Care to see how the Tortilla chips are made?

> *(***PEPPER*** takes* **DANNY***'s hand.)*

PEPPER. Let's go!

> *(They run off.)*

THE CROUPIER. Gemma, you want to know what it's like?

NARRATOR. SO, THEY WOULD LOSE OUT ON SUBSTANTIAL HOLIDAY EARNINGS FROM THE HYPED-UP PRODUCT.

GEMMA. ...LongWayHome, Jason-Jacuzzi-Bad-Idea, Valentine, and Paul Revere!

NARRATOR. OTHER AREA STORES,

BIGGER ONES WITH CORPORATE BACKING,

WOULD REAP THE BENEFITS OF NOT CLOSING EARLY FOR A TEAM BUILDING WILDERNESS EXPEDITION...

GEMMA. Or should we just put it all on Gemma's-on-Fire???

NARRATOR. BUT DON'T WORRY ABOUT OUR TIN CAT TROOPS,

NO ONE WILL REGRET TAKING OFF EARLY THAT DAY.

> (**CHEDDAR** *mimics the sound of a trumpet, the one it makes at the start of a horse race.*)

GEMMA. Do it – go!

> (**CHEDDAR** *takes off running.*)

THE CROUPIER. Gemma, care to drop the ball?

> (**THE CROUPIER** *holds the little Roulette ball up.*)

GEMMA. Moi?

THE CROUPIER. Oui.

GEMMA. Oui, oui!

Seriously Croup, what a day.

> (**THE CROUPIER** *hands the ball to* **GEMMA**.)

NARRATOR. NO ONE WILL REGRET THE ACTIONS TAKEN OR NOT TAKEN.

AS GEMMA HOLDS THE ROULETTE BALL UP TO THE LIGHT.

> (**GEMMA** *holds the ball up and smiles.*)

AS THE CROUPIER SPINS THE WHEEL

(**THE CROUPIER** *spins the Roulette Wheel.*)

AND GEMMA DROPS THE BALL INTO THE GAME

(**GEMMA** *drops in the little metal ball.*)

NARRATOR.
WHERE IT WILL GO
AROUND
AND AROUND

GEMMA.
It smells SO good in
here. Doesn't it?
Like potential.

AND AROUND
AND AROUND
AND AROUND

Did you know the bears
are waking up?

AND AROUND
AND AROUND
AND AROUND.

La Fin

Tin Cat Troop Song

(To be sung a cappella.)

Harnetiaux/Ware

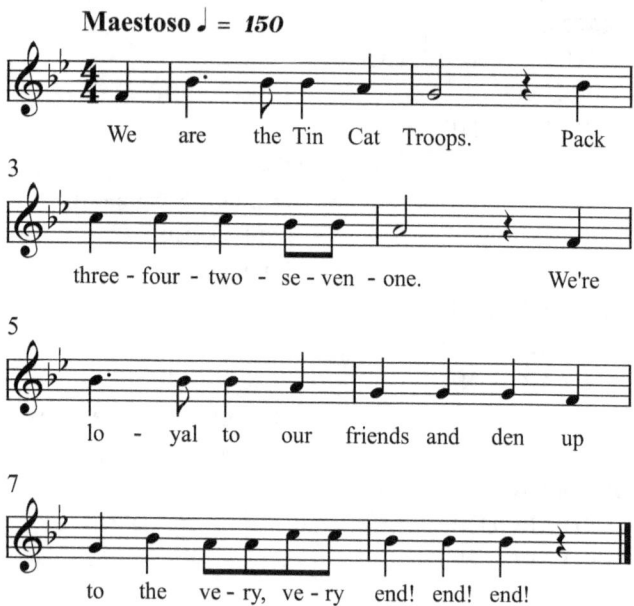

We are the Tin Cat Troops. Pack
three - four - two - se - ven - one. We're
lo - yal to our friends and den up
to the ve - ry, ve - ry end! end! end!

Tin Cat Fugue

(To be sung a cappella.)

Harnetiaux/Thomas

♩ = **210**

(Swing it; And definitely lose control by the end)

CHEDDAR:

Paul Re - vere is my horse,_

He's Grand-mas-ter of the_ course. A-ny suck-er with a

buck knows he is pure e - ques-tiran force. It's

CHEDDAR:

true, it's true. All the pa-pers say he's a

PEPPER:

My front-run-ner is Va-len-tine, she has got a

hul-la-ba-loo._ It's true, it's true.

great blood-line._ You can see by her pos - ture_

Bet on my life he'll ne-ver be glue.__ My

she has got a per-fect__ spine. So

CHEDDAR:
book-ie gave me an in-side__ tip:__ Paul Re-

PEPPER:
slick, so slick.

LUNCH:
What a-bout dar-ling E - pi - taph?__

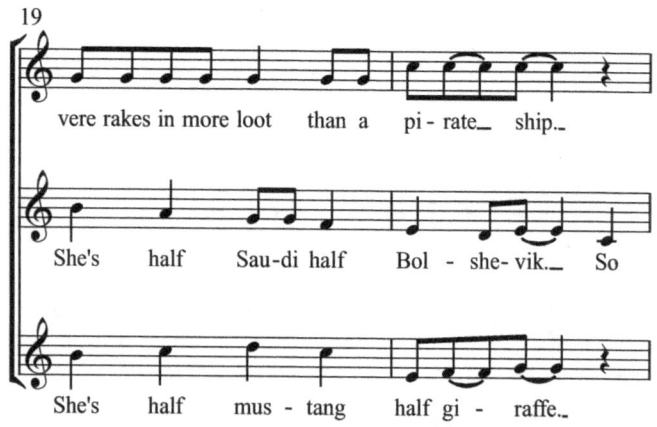

vere rakes in more loot than a pi-rate__ ship.__

She's half Sau-di half Bol - she-vik.__ So

She's half mus - tang half gi - raffe.__

21

Top voice: He's been known to shred the mor-ning line and

Middle voice: slick, so slick. She

Bottom voice: If you got a big ol' wad o' cash

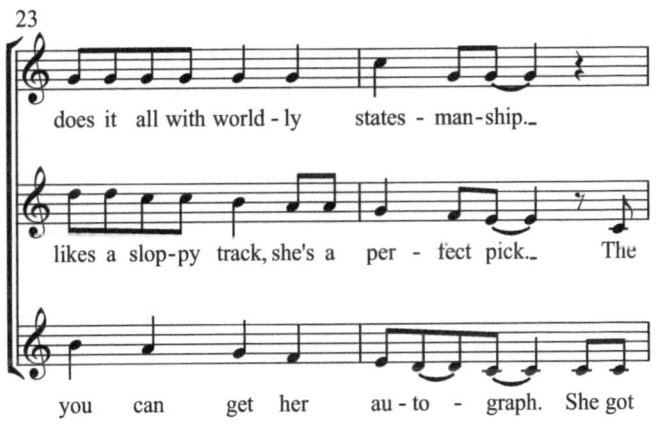

23

Top voice: does it all with world-ly states-man-ship.

Middle voice: likes a slop-py track, she's a per-fect pick. The

Bottom voice: you can get her au-to-graph. She got

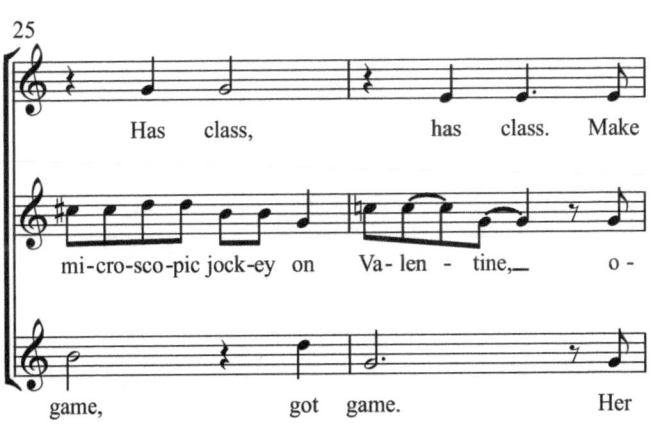

25

Top voice: Has class, has class. Make

Middle voice: mi-cro-sco-pic jock-ey on Va-len-tine, o-

Bottom voice: game, got game. Her

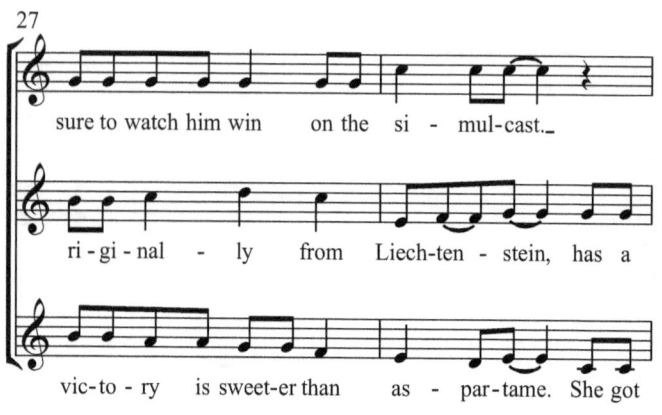

27

sure to watch him win on the si - mul-cast.

ri - gi - nal - ly from Liech-ten - stein, has a

vic-to - ry is sweet-er than as - par-tame. She got

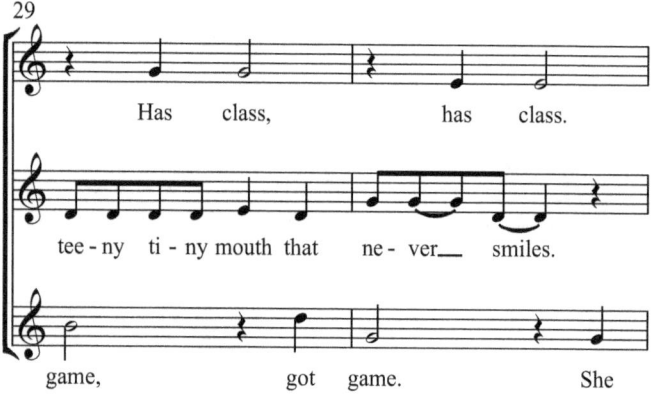

29

Has class, has class.

tee - ny ti - ny mouth that ne - ver__ smiles.

game, got game. She

31

Smokes the com-pe-ti - tion like mus - tard gas.

Kin - da looks like Doc-tor Frank-en - stein.

pays out more than an in - sur - ance claim.